CRASHING INTO JAKE

STRYKER SECURITY FORCE

SARA BLACKARD

Want to know how it all began? Find out what propelled Zeke and the team to create the Stryker Security Force by signing up for Sara Blackard's newsletter, and you'll receive **Mission Out of Control**, the *Stryker Security Force* prequel for FREE.

ONE

Chloe Rose leaned over the table and snagged a French fry from her cousin Piper's basket, striking when the server came and distracted Piper. Chloe put the end of the fry in her mouth and crunched the tip off. She closed her eyes and moaned as the salty goodness filled her mouth.

"I saw that." Piper cocked her eyebrow from across the table.

"I know, I know. They just looked so tempting." Chloe's shoulders slumped slightly as she placed the fry on a napkin.

"You'll get sick." Piper took a drink of water and glanced around to hide her concern, but Chloe still saw it in the way her cousin bit her lip. Piper wasn't very good at hiding her emotions.

"It's just a little taste, not even a real bite. I'll be fine." Hopefully. She took a gulp of iced tea to wash the possible poison down.

"I'm sorry, Chlo. I should've ordered the salad, too."

Piper glared at her pot roast sandwich like it was the devil.

If Chloe could eat it, she'd have the thing half gone by now. Of course, if her body didn't turn gluten into poison because of her severe celiac disease, the tempting plate wouldn't be so tantalizing. But then, the forbidden always drew people in.

"Stop. You know how I hate that." Chloe pointed her fork at Piper. "Eat that plate of goodness. Enjoy it, please. Besides, we can always stake out the grocery store later for some sinful treats we can both indulge in."

Piper smiled as she rolled her eyes. "You forget, I'm already cheating. I'm supposed to be eating healthy, not downing heart-attacks on a plate. I'll be eating salads for the next two weeks because of this bad boy." She lifted the dripping sandwich to her mouth and took a big bite. Her eyes widened, and she spoke around her food. "So worth it."

They both dissolved into giggles as Piper attempted to keep the bite from flying out of her mouth. Chloe hated that Piper thought she needed to eat healthy all the time, though she guessed she understood why. Being teased mercilessly as a kid for being a little on the heavy side would do that to a woman. Yet, Chloe failed miserably at keeping her jealousy over Piper's womanly curves and flowing dark brown hair stifled. Chloe yearned for, but probably would never have, curves men would drool over. Just mosquito bites for breasts and a flat backside. *Thanks for nothing, celiac.*

Most people didn't even give her celiac disease more than a "that sucks" thought. Not Piper. She was conscious of everything. She never brought gluten home to the apartment they shared. Rarely ordered gluten when they went out to eat. That was just one reason Chloe loved Piper so much. The fact that her sweet cousin had ordered the sandwich revealed how stressful the last few days had been on her.

Chloe relaxed into the booth seat and took a bite of her grilled chicken salad. When the director for the Winter Wondergrass music festival had called and begged her and her band to fill in for a last-minute cancellation on the main stage, it had been exactly what they needed. Any time she could get a gig, she jumped on it. There was no telling which one might catapult her budding career through the roof. It was a bummer they hadn't had enough time to scrounge up any other performances in the area. As Chloe's manager, Piper did wonders, but she wasn't a miracle worker.

Too bad the relief wasn't just for a fresh performance opportunity. Chloe shivered and turned her thoughts away from the odd messages being left on their business phone line. She and Piper were probably just overreacting. Chloe didn't have the fame to draw a stalker. Not yet, at least.

She loved the warmth that determination spread through her body. It drove her, had from the moment she'd lain in the hospital bed through most of her senior year with a diagnosis after years of being sick. Her body had cannibalized itself to the brink of death. It was amazing the destruction a microscopic protein could wreak.

"So, now that we're in beautiful Steamboat Springs,

Colorado for the next week, what the heck are we going to do?" Chloe ticked off the reality of the situation on her fingers. "It's cold as all get-out. We've never skied, never ice skated, never snowshoed. We have time to waste for once, but we're stuck in winter wonderland."

"It does pose a problem. Too bad we aren't more outdoorsy." Piper smiled at Chloe in the way that always got them into trouble as children. "There's supposed to be some good shopping downtown. You might need a new outfit for the concert Friday." She wiggled her eyebrows up and down.

Chloe loved shopping, and from the artsy-fartsy atmosphere they'd experienced in Steamboat so far, she could do some real damage here. While it might be superficial, there were some benefits to having parents that covered their inability to cope with her illness by giving her a ridiculously large trust fund.

Her parents hadn't ever really wanted kids, which was why they had stopped at one. Oh, they never came right out and said it, but leaving every summer for months of "business" vacations without Chloe had clued her in pretty quickly.

She'd had a pretty lonely childhood until Piper and her brother Davis came to live with her after their parents died. Having two more kids hadn't seemed to slow down her parents' travels. If anything, they'd been gone more. Then, when Chloe's illness had finally landed her in the hospital after years of being sick for no apparent reason, she'd felt the burden she placed upon her parents more heavily than ever before. They had always claimed she was being a hypochondriac just to get their attention.

Surprise, surprise when she ended up having a real-life chronic illness that almost killed her.

While her parents' money had given her the best care, it hadn't immediately fixed the problem. Then after she was better, her parents' relief that life was back to normal had been celebrated with a large bank account opened in her name.

Money fixed everything, at least to her parents' way of thinking. So while she wouldn't allow her father to buy her way into the music industry, she wasn't up to starving while doing it the good old-fashioned way. She'd already starved once in her life. She'd never do that again. Or have her closet suffer.

"Shopping it is." Chloe rubbed her hands in anticipation. "Forget about those calories you're so worried over. We're shopping so much they'll fall off."

"Ugh. I wish. My luck, we'll have to buy me a whole new wardrobe after this disaster."

Chloe rolled her eyes at Piper's comment about her food, while adrenaline rushed through Chloe's body at the opportunity her unsuspecting cousin had just given. "Just remember, you asked for it."

Piper's hand stopped halfway to her mouth, dropping ketchup from her fry to the table. "Wait. What? I think I missed something."

"A new wardrobe."

"Nope. Not going to happen. You know how much I hate trying on clothes." Piper shook her head and stuffed the fry into her mouth.

"Yes, dear cousin, but I also know you've been wearing the same handful of outfits for the last ten years."

Chloe leaned over the table to drive the point home. "I need my manager looking her best. You are my representative, right? If I have to play the part of country sweetheart, so do you."

The dowdy outfits that made Piper look frumpy had to go. She needed to realize what a hottie she was. Chloe's mission for the day became plain. Operation Piper Makeover would be in full effect as soon as they finished stuffing their faces.

When they ended their meals, Chloe dragged Piper to the rental car. She slumped dejectedly in her seat. Chloe ignored the pouting as she took off for Lincoln Avenue. The waitress had assured them they'd find plenty of shopping there.

Chloe whipped into a parking spot in front of a boutique and turned in her seat to face Piper. "I know you don't want to do this, but it's time. Please, just trust me. When have I ever steered you wrong?"

"What about the time you got me stuck in the elm tree?"

"That doesn't count." Chloe rolled her eyes. Piper always loved to bring that up.

"Or the time you convinced me to go skinny dipping, and my brother and Rafe caught us?"

Chloe cringed. Okay. That had been pretty bad. Especially since Piper had a major crush on her brother's best friend.

Piper took a deep breath and continued. "Remember the time—"

"Those times don't count and you know it." Chloe cut her off before she could continue the lengthy list of trouble. "You got me in a fair share of pickles when we were growing up as well. You know I'm talking about when it really matters. We've never let each other down. Ever. I promise I won't let you down now."

Nuts. She hadn't meant to get all emotional with her voice cracking and vision glazing over with tears. Chloe meant this to be fun. But the way Piper had a death grip on the door handle waved a big, red flag that fun didn't describe this activity. Chloe just wanted to see Piper finally get over the bullying she'd had to endure and embrace the amazing woman she was. Fancy clothes could never change a person, but it might just give her the confidence needed to see herself in a different light.

Chloe pushed Piper's hair behind her ear. "Come on, Pip. Let me show you what I see when I look at you."

Piper swallowed. "If I hate it, we don't buy a thing."

"Fair enough. If you love it, we have a bonfire with your old clothes as the fuel."

Piper turned away and narrowed her eyes at the boutique. She stuck her thumbnail in her mouth and bit it. Chloe prayed that her cousin would say yes, that Chloe could pay back a minuscule part of what Piper had done for her. Though clothes and a fresh look couldn't compare to the love and support Piper had always given, even when everyone else said Chloe wasn't well enough to chase her dream.

"Okay." Piper gave one firm nod. "But I get to light the match."

Chloe squealed and hugged Piper tightly over the console. "This will be so much fun."

"For you, maybe. For me it'll be torture," Piper countered, but Chloe didn't miss the suppressed smile behind the grimace.

"Come on. We're roasting marshmallows tonight."

"You do know you probably shouldn't roast food over burning clothes, right?"

Chloe shrugged. "Enough dawdling. We've got shops to conquer."

Three hours later, Chloe pulled into the drive of the house her father had insisted on renting for them when she'd told him of her gig. It was huge, with five bedrooms and more space than two people could ever use. It was ridiculous that her father also rented a different house entirely for the band, though it was nice to have this time with just Piper. Lately, the whole traveling band thing had taxed on her.

"Okay, I'm not sure if I can make it up the stairs to the door. My feet hurt that bad." Piper groaned in the passenger seat as she rotated her feet.

Chloe peered up the steps that earlier had seemed picturesque, but now looked like torture, and slumped. "Think we can get all the bags up in one trip?"

"It's worth a try. If we end up dropping some, at least they'll be closer than coming all the way back to the car."

Chloe popped the trunk, and they both threaded as many bags as their arms could carry. The straps cut into her muscle, and the load weighed so much she could hardly lift her arms. Maybe this wasn't such an excellent idea.

"Don't think. Just go." Piper nudged her toward the front door.

As they got to the bottom of the stairs, Piper's phone

started singing Mac Davis's old song, *It's Hard to be Humble.* Chloe laughed as Piper twisted to get into her handbag. Chloe wished she could reach her own phone just to take a video. Would the owners let them watch the security feed if this ended in an inevitable debacle?

"Just leave it. You can call him back." Chloe trudged up the steps.

"You know how hard it is to talk to my brother. I'll never get him again if I don't answer now." Piper grunted, then smiled in triumph as she pulled out her phone.

Calls from Piper's brother Davis were few and far between, with him being in the military. He tried to call every few weeks or so, but the time between calls had been closer to a month this time. After their parents had died in a car accident, the brother and sister had become closer than peas nestled in a pod. Missing a call was not an option for Piper.

"Hey, Davis. You're on speaker." Piper's breathless voice made Chloe chuckle.

"Hey, Pipster. What's got you panting like you just ran a mile?" Davis Field's smooth, low tone always soothed over Chloe's frazzled nerves.

It was too bad they didn't make more men like him. Then maybe finding someone who'd be willing to put up with her issues wouldn't seem so daunting.

"Shopping. Lots and lots of shopping." Piper panted.

"Chloe on a binge again?"

"Hey! I'll have you know most of this is Piper's."

She got to the top of the stairs and noticed a paper taped to the door. The managers must've needed to leave some paperwork or something. Piper's gasp and the thud of her bags dropping turned Chloe from the words written in marker she had started to read. Piper's face had turned white as the snow that surrounded them.

"Piper, what's wrong?" Davis's concern came through a second before Chloe opened her mouth to ask.

She lifted her trembling finger to the note. "He's found us."

"Who's found you? What's going on?" Davis practically shouted through the phone.

Chloe whipped her head back to the note, her eyes skimming over the words. Her stomach bottomed out, and she dropped her bags on the porch.

You think you can hide from me?

Chloe scrambled for the key to the door. Unlocking it, she pushed Piper in, then began chucking the bags they'd dropped into the entryway. As she stepped in, she ripped the note off the door and crumpled it into a ball. Perfect fire starter.

"Piper, talk to me now." Frustration edged Davis's normally calm voice.

"Chloe has been getting some strange text messages on our phone line for the band. We were hoping it was nothing, but it appears he followed us here to Colorado. He just left a note on the front door."

"Crap. Okay, listen. I have some friends who served in the Army with me that now run a security firm in Colorado. I'll call them and get them there as fast as possible." Davis's words came out rapid, like Chloe's heartbeat. "In the meantime, call the police and get them there. Maybe there's security footage of this guy."

"Okay. We'll do that." Piper nodded as she clung to the phone.

"No matter what, don't open the door to anyone unless you can read their badge number, or they give our password."

Piper turned wide eyes Chloe's way. "Okay."

"Love you, Pipster. You too, Chloe."

Piper stared at the black screen on the phone, the excitement of the afternoon that had lit her face leeching out to worry. Chloe turned to close and lock the door with a heavy heart. She'd done it again, brought that weight of apprehension on her cousin's shoulders. Maybe Chloe should just do like her parents wanted and live a quiet, safe life. Because if it wasn't her health, it was something else she did to cause the people she loved distress.

TWO

Jake Silva yanked his hand away from where he rubbed his knee. He'd twisted the prosthetic bottom half while playing chase with his boss's stepdaughter, Evangeline, earlier, and his knee still ached. The last thing he needed was for the others to witness him nursing it. The worry he'd see in the women's expressions would pinch, but it would be the guilt he saw in his brothers-in-arms that would turn Jake's contented mood dark.

"Uncle Jake, you stopped reading." Eva peered up at him from where she leaned against his side.

"Sorry, honey. I got distracted."

He'd already read *Beauty and the Beast* to her three times in the last thirty minutes, yet here he still sat, regaling the precious four-year-old of how Belle's love changed the beastly prince. He wished Eva still obsessed over *Sleeping Beauty*. That book didn't hit so close to home. It wasn't like the rambunctious girl to stay on one princess for long though, not when there were so many to choose from.

Eva ran her hand down the picture with a dramatic sigh. "What do you think your princess will look like?"

"My princess?" Jake forced his voice to not turn gruff. "I thought you were my princess."

Eva turned so she sat on her knees facing him, her little fists plopped on her hips. She screwed her face up into what he imagined she thought was mean, but really was just adorable. Man, he loved this girl. The last few months since she and her mother had showed up brought a light to the pit he'd spiraled into.

"Now you wisten to me, and you wisten to me now, mister." Where did she come up with this stuff? "You are a handsome prince, just like the beast."

She slammed her chubby finger on the picture of the beast hidden in shadows. He should stick to the shadows as well. Few wanted the reminder his scarred face gave. He shook his head and focused on Eva.

"Don't you shake your head at me. I need cousins and lots of them."

Jake choked on spit as he inhaled sharply. "Cousins?"

"Yes. If you get married, you'll have babies, then I'll get cousins."

"I don't think anyone will want ugly ol' me as a prince. Besides, I'm too cranky." He tweaked her nose, hoping to distract her. "But go tell Sosimo about your plan. He's already found and married his princess. You should tell them to hurry up."

Eva climbed onto his lap and put her tiny hands on both of his cheeks. The sorrow that pooled in her sparkling blue eyes nearly made him promise to rush off to wherever women hung out these days and round himself up a wife.

"You are not ugly or cranky. Don't talk mean like that. It's not nice."

What a jerk he was. "I'm sorry, sweetheart. I didn't mean to hurt your feelings."

"You're pretty and nice, and I love you, Uncle Jake." She threw her arms around his neck and squeezed tightly.

He held her and closed his eyes, glad for the moment to get the giant ball of emotion unstuck from his throat. The day his former Sergeant Major and now boss, Zeke Greene, had fallen and fallen hard for Eva's mother had been the day that hope for a new tomorrow peeked into his heart. While he still wasn't sure he could ever move past the ghosts that haunted him at night and be safe enough for a wife to be around, having women and children at the ranch helped him think less often of all he'd lost in the last mission he'd fought for the US Army.

One would think it would've done the opposite, since all he had ever wanted was to serve his country with honor and marry someone who would be his rock to come home to. It was a family legacy that had started with his grandfather, one he'd wanted more than anything. But one mission, one moment in time, had shredded all his dreams to dust. At least here he could live vicariously through his friends' lives, being a part of a family unit that had no blood ties.

Rafe rushed into the room, a crease marring his normally jovial face. "Hey, Fairy Princess, I need to steal

Uncle Jake away for important hero business. Why don't you go find Tina? I think she's working with that new dog of hers."

"Yeah!" Eva jumped in Jake's lap, kissing him loudly on his scarred cheek before jumping down and racing off. "Be safe, my brave knights."

"We will, my fair lady." Rafe waved to her and turned to Jake. "We're heading to Steamboat. Can you be ready to fly in ten?"

Jake nodded, his heart picking up with the intensity Rafe exuded. "What's up?"

"Davis Field just called—"

"From the sandbox?" Wasn't Davis still overseas?

"Yeah. His baby sister is in some kind of trouble." Rafe speared his hand through his normally perfect hair. "Well, I guess she's not a baby anymore, and it's more their cousin that's in trouble."

"Rafe, breathe, man. What do you know?"

"Some guy's been stalking Chloe, Davis's cousin. She's an up-and-coming country singer. She's in Steamboat for a music festival, and the creep followed them." Rafe headed toward the door. "You're flying us, and then you and I are playing babysitter."

Jake swallowed down his anxiety and followed Rafe out the door. He didn't mind his new job as part of Zeke's Stryker Security Force. Enjoyed it, surprisingly. The jobs he didn't like were the famous ones. They always looked at him funny, like they'd just bitten into a sour candy. Worst were the women that curled their bodies away in fear.

It shouldn't surprise him. Since his injury, he'd gotten that reaction from most women no matter where he went. No, Eva shouldn't get her hopes too high. He wouldn't be finding his princess anytime soon. Jake scowled as the joyful morning tanked to gloom.

THREE

Chloe tripped on a long skirt that dangled from the pile in her hands as she made her way down the stairs. Maybe she should've taken a smaller load? Or thrown the pile over the bannister. Yeah, that probably would've been smarter. Fewer trips up and down too. Not that Piper had that many clothes to bring down.

"What are you doing?" Piper gaped at her from the couch where she flipped through a magazine.

"Bonfire. Remember?"

"Now?" Piper stood, her voice coming out like a squeak.

"Yep."

"But what about the note? Shouldn't we stay inside and wait for Zeke's guys?"

Chloe tossed the clothes on the entry floor and rushed back upstairs. She would not cower in fear inside like some burrowed animal. Piper had enough worry for the both of them. Besides, Piper said the two men from Stryker Security should be there within the next hour or so, and there was no way Piper would light 'em up with guys around.

"Go pile those in the fire pit on the porch," Chloe hollered, making her way to Piper's bedroom.

Piper's muttering made Chloe chuckle, unwinding the tight ball her guts had twisted into. Piper's relay of the conversation with Zeke, the owner of Stryker Security, had helped too. He'd told them not to call the police until his men arrived. He wanted them protected before they let anyone in.

She hated that this jerk could make her fear even the police. She'd seen enough thrillers to know all it took was the right uniform and—boom—caught heroine. She gathered the rest of Piper's clothes and headed back downstairs just as Piper came from inside.

"I'm glad you already changed. Who knows what these friends of Davis's will look like?" Chloe wiggled her eyebrows as Piper blanched. "Why don't you run upstairs and get the rest while I stack this stuff up?"

Chloe had met enough of Davis's friends to know that the possibility of them being good-looking ranked high. She and Piper had too often whispered behind their hands when they'd visit Davis on base. It might be shallow, but she hoped they got some cute ones. If they liked to flirt, they'd get bonus points. It'd be a shame to have a boring protector. If she had to have one, she wanted one that kept things interesting.

She tossed the clothes on top of the fire pit and turned to find something to light the fire with. Wow, she definitely had watched *The Bodyguard* too many times in the hospital. The hospital had owned a handful of movies

CRASHING INTO JAKE   19

to choose from. Since the other four had been preschool cartoons, she and Piper had gotten really familiar with the romantic classic. In fact, they pretty much had it memorized. After Chloe had gotten back home, she'd sent the hospital a new library of movies.

She needed to remember that life never happened like it did in the movies, and she definitely wasn't gorgeous like Whitney Houston. She'd have to play it cool if she didn't want to come across as some ogling ditz. Maybe it'd be better if Zeke sent some happily married old guys.

"Okay. I also brought my grannie panties." Piper's cheeks pinked as she tossed them onto the pile. "No use keeping these with the insane amount of sexier ones you bought me. Not that anyone else but me will know."

"I'm telling you, pretty underwear builds confidence. And when you've snagged a guy and get married, he'll like them just as much as you do." Chloe whistled low and long. "Pip, you look stunning."

"Really? I feel ...fat."

"Don't even say that. Never again, Pip. You aren't. Not even close. You have all the right curves in all the right places." Chloe pushed on her cousin's shoulder. "Men will drool for miles. It's too bad you can't sing to save your life. With you on the cover, we'd sell millions."

"Whatever." Piper rolled her eyes and scrutinized the upcoming sacrifice.

Honestly, the fact that the purchase of new clothes transformed the wilting wallflower into an exotic orchid amazed Chloe. Piper's looks had always been beautiful, but the clothes she would choose left her skin colorless and her body shapeless. The deep red sweater she wore now made the gold of her dark brown eyes stand out. Too bad a new wardrobe couldn't transform Chloe. Nothing could help her curly blonde hair that celiac had thinned. Thank goodness she could pull off the pixie cut, otherwise she didn't know what she'd do with the stringy strands.

"Don't you think I should donate these clothes instead of burning them?" Piper bent to pull some shirts from the pile.

"Pip, you've been wearing these for so long, there's no way anyone else could fit to your mold."

"You're probably right." Piper bit her bottom lip. "I think we should start out with half and add more as they burn down, though." She glanced up at Chloe with a gleam in her eyes. "Wouldn't want to catch the house on fire. Firefighters and bodyguards all in one day might be too much eye candy to take in."

"You can never have too much eye candy."

They worked together to build the perfect pyre with the grannie panties at the top. Piper squeezed a long stream of starter fluid over the clothes and scrunched her forehead.

"Do you think that's enough?" Piper turned the can over in her hand and read the directions again.

"How should I know? Why don't you toss a match on, and we'll find out? If it doesn't catch, you could always squeeze more on."

Piper set the can down on the table and lit a match. "Goodbye, dear friends. Thanks for wrapping me in comfort all these years, but it's time to step out into a new me."

Chloe giggled as Piper bowed her head to the fire pit before tossing the match in. The whoosh of flames caused both women to shriek. Chloe's heart stopped in her chest then ramped up to hyper-drive as the flames settled down to a normal height. She peered at Piper, whose eyebrows almost touched her hairline, and burst out laughing. Good thing Chloe had short hair or more than clothes might've caught on fire.

Banging on the front door caused her to shriek again. Piper stepped around the fire pit to join Chloe next to the sliding porch door. Chloe gripped Piper's shaking extended hand.

"It can't be them yet. It hasn't been an hour," Chloe whispered. Ridiculous, since whoever rapped on the door couldn't hear her.

Another knock made her heart jump from hyper-drive to supersonic hyper-drive.

"What if it's him?" Piper's voice shook, steeling Chloe's spine.

This jerk wouldn't get the satisfaction of her cowering. He certainly wouldn't be pushing sweet Piper around. She already worried enough about Chloe's health.

"I hope it is. Then maybe I'll have a friendly talk with him. Introduce him to the lovely ski pole I found earlier."

Chloe marched to the front door, muttering to herself that she didn't need to fear a shadow. She peeked through the peephole to see two men. One had his back turned from the door and was scanning the area. The other scowled at the door like he could open it by sheer willpower. The tension from her shoulders relaxed. Surely these were the men from Stryker Security.

"What's the password?" Chloe cringed at the ridiculous saying that made her feel ten years old again. Her hope of a good impression slipped through her fingers, and she hadn't even opened the door yet.

The gruff man's deep voice sliced through the door like a hot knife through butter. "Butterfingers and potbelly pigs."

Her skin tingled. How did he make that sound sexy? *Focus, keep cool.* She unbolted the door while she chanted in her head. *You're not Whitney. You're not Whitney.*

The door felt like it weighed fifty pounds as she swung it open. Her gaze connected with the scowling man, and her knees wobbled. She may not be Whitney, but he knocked Kevin Costner out of the park. She stared, she knew it, but somehow couldn't tear her gaze away. His light blue eyes reminded her of the hydrangeas her mother had planted by the house. He had his hair pulled back into a low bun and a scruffy beard covered his face. He towered over her petite frame in an imposing way that should've made her feel frightened but didn't. His scowl deepened, and he scratched his cheek, drawing her attention to a large scar she couldn't believe she hadn't noticed.

"Chloe?" A familiar voice turned her head to the other man.

"Rafe?"

Rafe Malone squeezed her into a tight hug, causing

the other man to scowl even more. Davis's best friend sure had grown up. He'd always stolen hearts with his funny charm and playful good looks, one heart in particular, but those looks had turned him from boy-next-door to hubba hubba. She darted a glance back at Piper, who stood frozen by the couch. The color had leeched out of her face, leaving Chloe to wonder if the couch held her cousin up.

"Think we can move this reunion inside?" Tall, dark, and grumpy pushed Rafe on the back before scanning the neighborhood.

Rafe picked her up with a growl and stepped into the house. Nope, the Army hadn't trained the playfulness out of him completely. He placed her down and stepped back, his smile fading as he stared over her shoulder. He swallowed and cleared his throat.

"Pipster?" His voice pitched low and his eyes about bugged out of his head.

"Hey, Rafe. Long time, no see." Piper's voice came out calm and matter-of-fact, and Chloe almost cheered at her friend's ability to play it cool though Chloe knew Piper was probably on the verge of fainting.

"Too long, it seems." Rafe crossed the room and pulled her into a hug, lingering a tad long to Chloe's way of thinking. "You look amazing. Davis would flip a brick if he saw you now."

Chloe barely stifled a happy dance as she wiggled her eyebrows at Piper over Rafe's shoulder. Her makeover hadn't come at a more perfect time. Maybe now Rafe would notice what he'd been too dense to see as they grew up.

"Do I smell smoke?" The rich, low voice right behind her startled a squeak out.

She really needed to stop doing that. "Oh yeah, we were just ... um..."

The men marched to the back porch, completely zoned in on the threat out back. Piper whipped her frantic, pained face at Chloe. Shoot. Chloe rushed out behind the men to salvage the situation.

"I told you this was a terrible idea." Piper accentuated her told-you-so whisper with a jab to the ribs.

"It's fine. Just be cool."

"I've never been cool."

Piper's groan of despair fell all the way to Chloe's toes. She'd fix this. Somehow. The men stood frozen on the porch, staring at the smoking fire that had grown impressively tall since they'd lit it.

Rafe's partner tipped his head to the side. "Are those underwear?"

Piper wilted in Chloe's peripheral as she snatched up a handful of clothes left to burn and plopped them over the crown of perpetual embarrassment, smothering the flames to smoke. If Rafe hadn't changed from the jokester they knew growing up, Piper would never hear the end of it.

"Why are you two burning clothes? Some sort of demonstration or something?" Rafe coughed and waved the smoke from his face. He moved closer to Piper to get out of the fumes.

"It's a ceremonial pyre celebrating change." Chloe ignored the way Piper threw a glare at her.

"What change?" Rafe turned to Piper and scanned her up and down.

To Piper's credit, she didn't squirm.

"Well ... um ..." *Come on, Chlo, think.* "We didn't bring the right clothes for the Colorado cold, so we got new ones." She cringed at the ridiculous excuse.

"You got new underwear for the Colorado cold?" Rafe asked in a tone that clearly said he thought they were crazy, which he stressed with a snort.

She crossed her arms, determined to dry Mr. Chuckle Buddy's humor right up. "No, we found this store with some sexy bits of lace we couldn't pass up. No use keeping the cotton ones when you've got pretties to wrap yourself in. Though, I guess it's not really wrapping, since there's not much fabric there to begin with."

She cocked her head to the side and gave him a demure smile. He adjusted his coat that he hadn't taken off and cleared his throat. He peeked over at Piper. She stared into the fire while she rubbed the neckline of her sweater. She probably didn't realize the self-comforting act drew Rafe's stare like a moth to fire.

"But why the fire? Why not just throw them away?" Her unnamed protector's voice warmed her more than the now dying fire.

She tipped her head to the side at the impotent flames. Who would've known that clothes could smother a fire so completely? They may have to get the lighter fluid back out. She turned her attention back to Grumpy Guard and smiled.

She spread her arms wide, tipped her head back, and conjured up her most dramatic voice, which didn't take much conjuring at all. "Sacrifices to the Goddess of Fashion, petitioning her for marvelous fits that drive men—"

The fire whooshed into an impressive shot of flames. Chloe yelped and stumbled backward as blazing fingers licked her face. The pile of clothes still waiting to perish wrapped around her foot and tripped her. This backward tumble would hurt. She cringed as she braced for impact.

Arms of solid steel wrapped around her and pulled her against an equally powerful chest. A comforting scent of spices, oranges, and the woods wafted from him. She looked up into eyes that weren't glaring but held concern. She was so pulling a Whitney. Crushing on your bodyguard proved too easy to avoid.

"I've got you." His words curled her toes.

Oh boy, you do.

His eyes widened before his scowl slammed back into place. Did she just say that out loud? She cringed as he righted her. Maybe she shouldn't have thought about that stupid movie so much this last hour. Maybe then her brain would keep thoughts in instead of words out.

Besides, Whitney and Kevin's story ended with no one happy. She'd had enough of that to last two lifetimes. She dreamed of strong arms around her through years of life, not just a moment, and children's laughter as the soundtrack. So instead of fantasizing about how Kevin Costner held Whitney to slow dance, she needed to replay the end with him all alone. Maybe then she'd keep her perspective straight.

FOUR

Jake glanced out the sliding glass door at Chloe and Rafe on the back porch. Piper had excused herself into the kitchen where she chopped vegetables with a vengeance after the whole bonfire incident, while Chloe sat staring at the small flames that devoured the last of the burnt offering. Rafe chatted with her, probably making some kind of joke. Chloe tipped her head back and laughed. Her pixie form was contrary to the hearty sound that flipped his stomach. He scowled and continued watching the security footage the rental company had sent over.

He didn't need his stomach acting like he hadn't moved past high school. He definitely didn't need to focus on the way her dark blue eyes had appeared almost violet as they'd looked up at him in surprise.

The moment she'd opened the door, looking like a beautiful fairy princess, he'd known she'd cause issues. No one could look like a gorgeous version of Tinkerbell and not be trouble with a capital T. Everyone knew fairies created nothing but mischief.

Jake clenched his jaw as another laugh floated into the living room and focused on the screen before him. Case in point, she sat outside with no regard to her safety while her cousin worked hard in the kitchen. Chloe about lit the porch on fire with her ridiculous bonfire of toxic flammables. She also hadn't flinched, pulled away, or cowered when she had met him. He scoffed. He shouldn't list that last one on the negative side, but he couldn't help it. Seeing her reaction as anything but negative would only keep his twisting gut in nervous knots he couldn't afford to have. Not while on a case. Maybe never.

He leaned closer to the screen as a figure strolled along the sidewalk and turned into the driveway. Darn it. He hoped the man had driven so they could know what vehicle to look for. The guy wore a black North Face coat with the hood pulled over his head. The bill of a ball cap stuck out of the hood, completely throwing his face in shadow. Jake had nothing but a build and a black jacket hundreds of others in this town probably had.

He switched over to the other feed that shot from a different angle across the street and cued it to the correct time. He scrutinized the video as the man walked up to the door. When the stalker turned to scan the houses, something caught Jake's attention. He rewound the feed and slowed it down. His hands and foot tingled with the additional level of threat. He rubbed his leg below the knee, where the prosthetic connected, and whistled. Rafe's head snapped to Jake. With a single nod, Jake had Rafe and Chloe in the living room.

"What'd you find?" Rafe slid and locked the patio door.

"A stalker."

Jake tried to ignore how the crease in Chloe's forehead made him want to smooth it away with promises of safety. Maybe a kiss or two on her plump lips—Jake shook his head to clear it of stupidity. He'd never had a problem staying on track, and he didn't want it off track with a pampered country star used to getting everything she wanted.

Jake frowned at the screen, the unfair assessment poking his conscience. She had done nothing to get such judgement from him, not really. In fact, he admired how she drew their attention from the pile of Piper's clothes to herself to relieve some embarrassment that had splashed across her poor cousin's face. Her off-hand comment of lacy underwear and her lack of fright over him screwed with his brain, making him wonder things he shouldn't.

She sat next to him on his scarred side, the couch barely dipping with her slight frame. He wished he hadn't pulled his hair back off his face. Now she'd get a good look at his scar, and her friendly demeanor would fade.

"You found him?" She leaned forward and squinted at the screen.

"Yeah, though the video doesn't show much." He clicked the button to play, trying to ignore that she smelled like some jungle flower.

Chloe leaned forward a little more toward the screen like she tried to get a better look, then shook her head as she crossed her arms and flopped back against the couch.

Her arm brushed his as she shifted to curl her feet up onto the cushion. The contact spread warmth to his shoulder. What in the world? He cleared his throat and forced himself not to move away.

"If I zoom in, we can kind of see his face in the shadows. Recognize him?" He turned to Chloe, who had pulled her knees up to her chest.

She stared at the screen, her eyes wide in her delicate face. Her laughter and spirit seemed to drain with the little color she had left in her pale face. She shivered, pulled her knees closer to her, and shook her head.

"Piper, do you recognize this guy?" Rafe motioned Piper over from the dining room table where she'd just placed a steaming dish.

Jake leaned back against the couch, debating if he should move or not. Chloe had sat so close that mere inches separated them. He didn't want her uncomfortable with his presence. She leaned into him, and her shoulders relaxed. The slight motion unfurled something in his gut.

Rafe spun the computer so Piper could get a look. A vertical line creased her forehead as she leaned toward the computer. She pulled her bottom lip in between her teeth and tipped her head to the side. Jake hid his smirk as he watched Rafe stare at her lips and swallow. Oh man, Davis would flip if he knew his best friend had found a new appreciation for his baby sister.

"It's so dark, I can't really tell. There's just too much of his face covered." She sighed and straightened. "Sorry."

"Don't be sorry, Pipster." Rafe stepped to her, gave

her a one-armed hug across the shoulders, then practically jumped away and crossed his arms. "I don't think I could recognize my mother in that instance."

Piper smiled up at him before ducking her head and pulling her hair behind her ear. "I better finish getting dinner on the table."

"I'll help." Rafe followed her to the kitchen.

A giggle pulled Jake's gaze to Chloe. The pink had returned to her cheeks. Her eyes sparkled with laughter.

"What?"

She pointed her chin toward the kitchen. "Rafe doesn't stand a chance."

He stared back into the kitchen where Rafe's full attention stayed glued on Piper. "Might be right about that."

"Hopefully."

She sighed next to him. A comfortable silence settled around them. Jake couldn't remember the last time he'd felt so at ease next to a woman. He hadn't, not since that messed up mission.

"Jake?" Her soft whisper pulled his gaze to her.

She peered up at him. A firmness had replaced the fear. She leaned forward, her expression intent. He swallowed the anxious lump in his throat.

"That man had a gun holstered to his side, didn't he?" Her tone warned him not to lie. Not that he would.

"Yeah."

Her gaze darted into the kitchen before she leaned even closer and pitched her voice lower. "Don't tell Piper. She already worries too much. This would throw her over the edge."

"You want me to lie?"

"No. Just ... if she didn't notice it herself, she doesn't need to know. It changes nothing." Chloe laid her hand on his arm, spreading that warmth back up his shoulder. "Ever since her parents died, she's anxious about those she loves leaving her. Davis going off to play hero gives her enough stress for three people. Then you add me into the mix, and she's wound so tight with nerves, I'm surprised she can function. I don't want to cause her more worry than I already have."

How could she be more concerned for her cousin's emotions when the guy after her carried around a gun? It blew his perception of her right out the window.

He nodded. "Okay, I'll let Rafe know not to tell her ... for now."

Her smile almost blinded him. "I'm glad Dictator Davis called you. Thanks for being here."

She leaned over and gave him a quick kiss on his scarred cheek before hopping up and rushing into the kitchen. He balled his hand into a fist to keep from rubbing the rippled skin that tingled from her touch. She rubbed Rafe's hair, messing up his perfect style with a burst of laughter. She was trouble, all right. If he didn't watch himself, he'd end up like Rafe, without a chance in the world to keep his thoughts where they should stay. As much as he longed to find someone that lit the fuse to his heart, he couldn't afford that kind of distraction. Not until he could control the beast that emerged each night in his nightmares.

FIVE

"Can you believe Jake's making us move? Ugh. He's an absolute beast." Chloe tossed more clothes into her suitcase as she exited her closet.

"No, he's not, and you know it." Piper grabbed the pile of clothes off the suitcase and began folding the items.

Chloe spun and stomped back into the closet. She hated that Piper told the truth. Jake wasn't a beast at all, even though he said little and scowled too much. Her fear of the situation had her lashing out at the person running the *Let's Protect Chloe* show. She hated the ice that had settled in her gut since seeing that gun strapped to the creep's waist. She huffed and threw the last of her clothes in the suitcase, snagging the stuff Piper wanted to fold and zipping the mess closed.

"You're right. He's not a beast." Chloe flopped on the bed.

"Of course, I'm right." Piper flipped her hair over her

shoulder and winked. "Maybe your panties are in a wad because he's smoking hot."

Chloe's heart rate picked up, and she stifled a smile. "He's okay."

Piper snorted, tossing a shirt Chloe had missed in her stuffing. "Whatever. I can see right through you, dear cousin."

"Fine, he's gorgeous, and his voice makes my toes curl." Chloe threw her arm over her eyes. "But it doesn't matter what I think of him, Piper. You know that. I have too many problems for any sane man to sign on to."

"You're delusional. Any guy would be lucky to have you." Piper came around the bed and flopped next to her.

"No, Piper, I'm realistic. Who would ever want to get involved with a china doll? I can't think of anyone who'd want that headache."

"It's not that bad. You have your celiac under control now."

"Think about it. He takes a drink of a beer or eats a sandwich, then gives me a kiss and—wham—I'm out for three days. And what about the possibility that I may never have kids? No man will ever want to mess with that." She sat up as all her old insecurities rose to strangle her. "Men want strength, not frailty. They want to see their woman plump with child so they can beat their chest and grunt in satisfaction, not have to curl up each night to someone who can hardly keep any weight on their scrawny bones."

"You don't give yourself enough credit." Piper grabbed Chloe's hand and squeezed. "You have more strength than anyone I know. I would've given up in that hospital after fighting as long as you did. But you, you barged through it with sunshine and determination. If you can't get pregnant, who cares? Think of all the children you could adopt."

Chloe shook her head and tried to stand.

Piper tightened her grip and shook her arm. "Get out of your head, Chloe Rose Fields. Any man who wouldn't see you as the gift you are is an idiot."

Chloe rolled her eyes and kissed Piper on the cheek. She laid her head on Piper's shoulder, digging up the kernel of hope her cousin's words planted. Chloe had no room for silly dreams in her heart. If her own parents could see nothing but her illness when they now looked at her, no one would ever see more either. They'd be foolish to. No, Chloe couldn't let hope take root, no matter how dangerously gorgeous Jake looked or how when she had sat next to him her nerves had settled into a peaceful harmony.

A knock on the doorjamb pulled both their heads around. Jake shifted on his feet and cleared his throat. Had he heard her little whinefest? She sure hoped not. He didn't need another reason to think her crazy. She pressed her lips together to stifle the smile the image of the underwear burning caused.

"We got us a place that's more secure. We'll be leaving in ten if you think you'll be ready." Jake's deep voice made the hair on her neck stand up.

He stared straight at her with a look that pooled white-hot lava in her belly. Dang, it should be illegal to have such an effect on her. If Kevin Costner would've had half of Jake's looks, Whitney would've been putty in his hands, not a spoiled brat.

"Yeah, sure." Was that her voice? Hopefully, he didn't hear the pathetic way it'd gone all husky.

He nodded, then turned down the hall, his footsteps fading as he left. How could she keep the bodyguard at arms' length when his stares made her want to agree to whatever he said? *Want us to hide in a bunker until the show? Sure, thing. It sounds romantic. Can I bring candles? Want to fly me away and lock me in a tower? Absolutely, where's the plane?* She shook her head.

Piper whistled. "Was that tension or was that *tension*? Did you see the way he looked at you? I got all hot and bothered, and he didn't even gaze at me as if he'd like to eat me up."

"That was nothing more than a do-what-I-tell-you look." Chloe pushed on Piper's shoulder and stood, though the memory of his look was kind of steamy.

"Yeah, right. If you really believe that, you should get out more. Even I, who has dated no one, knows what that look was."

"Hey, just because the love of your life suddenly sauntered in and can't seem to keep his eyes off you, doesn't mean that we'll all get our happily ever after." Chloe probably shouldn't dig, but she had to know what Piper thought.

"Now who's seeing things? Rafe hasn't looked at me any different from how he always did. Besides, he's still just a big kid." Piper shoved the shirt in the front zipper and lifted the suitcase off the bed. "I probably shouldn't hold my breath for him. I'll just end up passing out."

Piper rolled the suitcase out into the hall, her shoulders slumped. Men sucked. Why did she and Piper let themselves get all twisted up over their lack of relationships? The afternoon had gone so great with Piper turning a corner on the road to increased self-esteem. Now, she'd slammed into reverse with her inability to see Rafe's attraction. Chloe would just have to do something about that. She wouldn't let Piper think wrongly about herself any longer. She smiled as she surveyed the room once more to make sure she didn't forget anything.

Piper was right about one thing. Chloe had survived almost dying. She may not be strong in body, but she was strong in spirit. She hadn't cowered away from her disease, and she sure as shooting wouldn't cower from this creep. Their bodyguards would just have to stay on their toes, because she wouldn't be bullied into hiding. She didn't fight her way through the valley of death to not live fully in the land of the living.

SIX

Jake followed closely behind Rafe in the other vehicle to their new location. Relief had loosened his limbs when Zeke had found the place away from the mainstream. While the homes were beautiful and convenient at the base of the ski slope, they also had built them with small yards. The tight neighborhood had made his skin crawl with their limited field of sight. This new place not only had an impressive security system, but the houses were spaced apart. He hoped the move shook the stalker off until the concert. If he couldn't find them, he wouldn't pose an immediate problem.

Jake squeezed the steering wheel as he watched their six through the side mirror. When he still saw no one following, he released his grip. He could feel Chloe's gaze on him as they stopped at a red light.

"So, Jake, how long have you known Rafe?" Her cheerful voice tinkled over him like lyrical notes.

She must be an incredible singer with the way her

voice slid right through him. Since he'd overheard her talking to Piper, it seemed his nerves couldn't stop firing. He hadn't meant to eavesdrop. He'd just paused outside in the hall to get the disappointment from her calling him a beast pressed down so he wouldn't growl. After hearing his voice made her toes curl, his throat had dried right up, afraid to break whatever strange spell had been cast on her. Women didn't find him gorgeous, not anymore, and his voice would make her toes curl for an entirely different reason if she heard him shouting at night from his dreams.

"I met Rafe my third year in. We were both in the training program for the team together."

He hadn't gotten rid of the lug yet. Not that he would want to. Rafe and the others had become his brothers he'd never had.

"So you were on the Special Ops team too?" Her big eyes widened even more. "That's impressive."

He shrugged. Impressive would be walking away whole. Though he doubted any of them had.

"How long were you enlisted?"

"I joined up when I turned eighteen and served for nine years."

"Wow, that young?" Chloe leaned her back against her door to watch him, making him feel like a bug under a magnifying glass.

"Family tradition." Did his voice sound odd, or was he just paranoid?

"That's cool. Your dad was in the Army then?" Her question held a cheerful tone.

"Dad, grandpa, great-grandpa. As far back as the

Revolution, my family can trace our military life." *Shoot. Don't get all sentimental, Silva.*

"Why'd you get out?" Her words crashed his sentimentality to the floorboard.

"I was injured."

"Oh." She cleared her throat. "You look fine now, better than fine."

In his peripheral, he saw her grimace and roll her eyes. Her unease made his mouth tweak until he remembered where the conversation had led. He clenched his jaw.

"Yeah, well, the Army doesn't have much use for a one-legged man." He glanced into his side mirror so he wouldn't have to see her reaction.

"That's a load of horse dung. With prosthetics these days, you can do anything you did before." She crossed her arms. The force of her objection had his limbs tingling.

She glared at him like he would debate her. Normally he would, but her tone bound the words in his throat. Why would she care if the Army could use him or not?

"If you want to stay in the Army, they shouldn't make you get out." She motioned her hand up and down his body. "You saved me without a bit of hesitation."

"Catching pixies as they fall is different from battle." He grinned at her, the push of his cheeks feeling foreign.

When had he flirted last? Not that he'd flirted with her. At least, he shouldn't, but she surprised him with her defense of him.

She shrugged and gazed out the front window. "You seem strong enough to me."

He balled his fist on his thigh so he wouldn't rub his injured leg that itched from her off-handed compliment. Jake didn't know what to do with her. Most people had a moment of pity before they did their best to ignore the obvious, pretend it didn't exist. It hadn't even fazed Chloe. She seemed mad someone would think badly of him.

"I have some plans for this week before the concert. We'll have fun while we're here." Chloe rubbed her hands in a gleeful motion.

He peeked over at her. Were her compliments just a ploy to soften him up and get him to do what she wanted? He shook his head and turned his focus back out the windshield. She didn't seem like the type. Then again, he didn't know her at all.

"That depends." He glared forward.

"Nope. We can be smart about it, but I'm not living under a rock because of some jerk."

"A jerk that carries a gun." Thankfully, he'd brought enough of June's Supersuits for the four of them, but it wasn't foolproof.

"That part is unfortunate." She tapped her finger to her cheek. "I already have something booked tomorrow, but I don't think it'll be a problem."

He rolled the tension from his shoulders and tried not to sound irritated. "What's that?"

She turned to him with pure joy filling her face. "I've booked us hot-air balloon rides."

"What?"

"This company does hot-air balloon rides through the valley. I've always wanted to go up in one but never have.

I saw the advertisement in the visitor magazine back at the house. I couldn't believe they were available for tomorrow."

"You realize it will be freezing, right?"

She waved his complaint off. "We packed winter gear. Besides, the cold will be worth it to experience something like that."

He thought about the logistics of an outing like that, and his shoulders relaxed. It shouldn't be hard to keep her safe. Most of the time would be up in the air, far from reach. Too bad they couldn't stay in a balloon all week. If she picked activities like this, having outings shouldn't be too hard.

"The day after tomorrow, we have lunch with the event director at a sponsor restaurant, and then I wanted to surprise a board member's daughter with a visit. She's the one who got me the gig. She also has celiacs and has to be homeschooled because her reaction is severe like mine."

"Any chance we could change the lunch to our place? Maybe have the kid come out too?" Jake hadn't even stopped speaking before her head shook.

"This is a publicity event, a chance to show I'm excited to be here for this show. I have to do what I can to schmooze these guys. It's amazing how connected this business is. If I rub one person the wrong way, my career stays in the dive bars, making nothing." She crossed her arms and glared at him. "I can't risk that."

"Why don't you just start your own label? From what Rafe said, you could afford to. Why go through all of this?" Jake turned into the driveway, rolling down his window to punch in the code to close the gate behind them.

When he pulled his head back into the car, she pounced. "Haven't you ever wanted to feel like you earned something? That you deserve your success because you worked for it and could be proud of that? I don't want to buy my way into this business. That's cheating."

"I get that." He glanced at her as he pulled up to their new place. "But there are many people who produce their own music, that whole indie movement and all. Just because you can afford to pay for things others may not, doesn't mean its cheating. People still have to buy your music."

"I just don't want the reason I make it to be because of my daddy's money."

"I don't doubt you'll make it, one way or another. You have the spunk." He put the car in drive and turned to her. "But think about this for a second. What if your daddy's money could not only help you, but help others as well? I can imagine it's a fierce battle getting discovered in the music business. But if you could record on your own without a label and make it, couldn't you then help other artists do the same?"

She stared at him a moment, and he shifted under the scrutiny. Why in the world was he talking so much? He didn't care what she did with her career. She pulled one side of her bottom lip between her teeth as she thought. He broke out into a sweat. He needed to remember, in the future, that talking to the clients just caused issues.

She tempted him to do things he shouldn't, like

wondering how she'd react if he leaned over and kissed her. If his progress with his PTSD kept plugging at the speed he currently went, years would pass before he felt in control enough that something wouldn't trigger a reaction out of him. He couldn't ask a wife to go through the nights with him. He'd heard enough horror stories around the base to not take his condition lightly. The possibility that he'd thrash in the night and hurt his wife or worse, wake up with his hands around her throat, scared him to celibacy. Until an outgoing pixie, that is. Now it seemed his mind's opposition wavered, thinking kissing said pixie might be a new venture worth exploring.

"You know, that's a thought with merit." She patted his arm. "Thanks, Jake."

He knew it was and glanced at her lips. Wait, what was she talking about? Oh, yeah, her music. "I'm here to help."

He pushed open the driver's door before he did anything that got his mind thinking crazy thoughts. This week could prove too much for him. They might need to call in back-up. He looked at the petite woman as she attempted to yank her hundred pound suitcase from the trunk. Then again, if he called more guys in for a job so small, he'd never hear the end of it. He'd just have to rein those errant thoughts in and remember why he couldn't subject a woman to his problems.

SEVEN

Chloe bounced on her toes as she stepped out of the vehicle and watched the hot-air balloon company set up for their rides. With it only being seven in the morning, the sun hadn't risen above the mountains high enough to warm everything up. She'd have to remember to thank Jake for the thin suit he'd made both her and Piper put on under their clothes. He claimed it was some kind of armor, which seemed ridiculous with how thin it was. The fabric, tight against her skin, helped keep her warm, so at least it did something.

The frosty air bit at her cheeks and made her nose run. She sniffed and smiled at Jake as he stepped up next to her. His face turned down into the frown she had become accustomed to. She rolled her eyes and squeezed her arms close to her body, adjusting her camera she'd hung from her neck and taking a drink from the steaming matcha tea latte they'd gotten on the way.

Piper rounded the back of the vehicle with her face scrunched up. Chloe hoped her cousin wouldn't kill her when she found out what she had done. If she played it right, no one would pick up on her ploy.

Piper pointed with her coffee cup between the two balloons. "Looks like someone else is going up too."

Here goes nothing. "Well, actually, that one is ours as well."

All three of them turned to her with different expressions of confusion. She cringed, hoping to give off a genuine I-messed-up look. A bird twittered in the brush and cheered her on.

"Actually, I booked both of them." She pretended to be embarrassed by motioning with her chin to the closest balloon. "I didn't realize the baskets were that big."

Piper's head whipped back to the balloons, glancing between the two of them. Rafe smirked and shook his head, taking a deep drink from his coffee as he scanned the surrounding field.

"We'll cancel one of them." Jake's deep voice pulled her attention to him.

Don't ruin this, Mr. Grumpy. "That would be silly. They're already paid for. Besides, it would be rude to cancel now after they've already set up."

"I don't like it." Jake secured his hands on his hips in a typical take-charge stance.

"What's not to like?" Chloe hugged her arms to her body and took another sip. "There's two of you, two of us, and two balloons. No one will be left alone, and no one can snatch me up there."

Jake crossed his arms and turned in a circle, looking at the landscape. "It's too exposed. Anyone could watch you."

"Today is the perfect day for this." She took a step closer when he scowled. "Think about it. My stalker probably doesn't know where we've moved to yet. Probably has no clue we're even here at the butt crack of dawn. And even if he saw us up there once we've taken off, how would he ever know it's us?"

Jake shook his head and looked up to the sky. If Chloe didn't act fast, she'd lose the fight. She had to give Piper this chance alone with Rafe. After the concert finished, Piper might not see Rafe for another five years.

Chloe stepped closer and leaned up against the only hitch in her plan. "Please go on a balloon ride with me." She batted her eyes for extra measure, hoping her silliness won him over.

He peered down at her. His light blue eyes matched the early morning sky. Dang, her flirting was affecting her more than it seemed to affect him. Her arm tingled where it leaned up against him. Something about the way he stared into her eyes anchored her to him and faded all silliness away.

He swallowed and tore his gaze away, breaking whatever trance he'd just put her in. "Fine. But from here on out, we set up outings together."

He stepped away from her to grab something out of the vehicle. Chloe let the air that had bottled up in her lungs out in a whoosh. She shook her head. *Keep your wits, Chlo, before you make an even bigger fool of yourself.*

She stepped up next to Piper, whose face seemed paler than normal. She jumped when Chloe bumped her shoulder against her cousin's. Chloe smiled and wrapped her arm around Piper's waist.

"Come on. Let's get closer and watch them air up the balloons. It might be warmer." Chloe pulled Piper's arm, but she didn't move.

Piper's coffee cup trembled in her hands. She couldn't be afraid. This was the woman who dragged Chloe on ride after ride when the carnival came through every year. Chloe frowned and laid her head on Piper's shoulder.

"Pip, what's wrong?"

"Nothing." Piper forced a fake smile.

"Piper."

"I don't know, okay? Something about all of this ..." She motioned toward the balloons. "Gives me the heebie-jeebies."

"This scares you, yet you'll go on thirty-year-old carnie rides that probably have more rust than metal?"

"They aren't that bad." Piper huffed and set her coffee on the bumper. "Think about it. We get up there, and the only thing between us and a million-foot drop is a thin piece of fabric. What if a bird flies into it and rips it?"

"Exaggerating a bit?"

"Maybe."

"Okay. Why don't we go talk to those guys setting up about it, maybe get a closer look at the balloon?" She hugged Piper's shoulder. "I think you'd be upset with yourself if you didn't go, though."

Piper heaved a heavy sigh. "Yeah, you're right."

Chloe placed her cup next to Piper's, grabbed her hand, and pulled her toward the loud fan that blew into the closest balloon. It billowed the balloon wide open, allowing the scorching air from the gadget to blow in. The fire burned loud like a thousand blowtorches, and her toes danced in her boots with excitement. She skipped a couple of steps, then turned to walk backward so she could face Piper.

"Besides, why pass up this opportunity to be alone with Rafe?" Chloe wiggled her eyebrows.

"Shh." Piper grabbed Chloe's arm and pulled her close, pushing a laugh out of Chloe's chest. "Are you crazy? He'll hear you."

"So?"

"So, the only way Rafe Malone has ever seen me is as Davis's baby sister."

"Trust me, he's not thinking you're a baby anymore." Chloe wrapped her arm around Piper's waist so she couldn't bolt and continued walking toward the balloon. "A babe, yes. A baby, definitely not."

They both turned their heads to where Rafe talked with Jake. When he smiled and nodded at Piper, she snapped her head back forward. Chloe squished her lips together to keep her smile contained.

"I am not allowing you to get my hopes up here," Piper hissed.

"It's just a little balloon ride, Pip. Don't think too much about it."

Chloe pulled Piper to the good-looking man helping set the balloon up and asked how tough the balloon was. The question seemed silly to her, because a bird wouldn't possibly fly into something so big. After she got the ball rolling, Piper quickly took over, asking a million questions Chloe had never even thought about.

The man laughed and put his hand out to Piper. "Come here, and I'll show you."

She tentatively placed her hand in his, and he pulled her towards the balloon. Chloe gave her a thumbs up and waved her on when Piper turned around with a shocked look on her face. Piper couldn't even blame this special attention the man showered on her on the new wardrobe since it was hiding under her snow gear. Chloe would have to point out later that the man's attention had everything to do with Piper's beauty.

"What's he doing?" Rafe's voice caused her to jump.

His rough tone had her peeking up at him. He'd crossed his arms over his chest and a scowl she'd never seen before wrinkled his face. Chloe almost danced at Rafe's obvious jealousy. This might work out better than she hoped.

"Piper's a little nervous about going up, so that nice-looking guy is showing her around the balloon to ease her mind." Chloe kept her gaze trained forward so she didn't blow it.

"He's not so nice looking." Rafe smoothed his hand over his hair, and Chloe almost hooted in triumph.

Now to go in for the kill. "Listen, Rafe, Piper's pretty scared about this."

"Pipster? She loves rides." A line of concern formed between his eyebrows.

"Yeah, I know. Surprised me, too. Do you think you can keep an eye on her while you're up there? I don't want her to pass out or anything."

He nodded and rubbed his hands together. "Yeah, I'll keep a real close eye on her."

Chloe let her smile free. "Thanks, Rafe." Her mood turned serious. "I'm glad you're here. Piper takes on so much. It'll be good for her to have a little Rafe magic around."

Rafe rubbed his chest and nodded. The balloon filled with more hot air, drawing her attention. She watched in awe as the furnaces on both balloons fired in a long steady rush and expanded the colorful fabric into the air. Chloe couldn't contain her excitement and cheered as the beautiful rainbow spheres filled completely. Piper made her way back to where Chloe stood with Jake and Rafe, talking lively with the worker.

When Piper stepped up next to them, Rafe put his arm over her shoulder and looked down at her. "You okay?"

Piper ducked her head and shrugged. "I am now."

"All right, I think we're ready to go. You two will be in the far balloon." He pointed to Piper and Rafe. "I'll be your pilot."

"Great," Rafe muttered next to Chloe.

"You two will be with Ted in this baby." He motioned to Jake and Chloe, then at the basket right behind him.

He droned on for about five minutes on safety and balloon mechanics, which Chloe tuned out. The sun had finally peeked over the mountains, and she wanted to fly with it. When the man finally said to load up, she practically ran to the basket before her.

She stepped up onto the stool and tried to swing her leg over. Four more inches on her five-foot frame and she could do it, but genetics hadn't blessed her with height. Hadn't blessed her with much, period. She scanned the basket for something to leverage her foot on when large hands wrapped around her waist.

"Here, let me help you." Jake's breath blew across her neck as he stepped close.

Warmth spread from her waist to her neck. If the heat that rushed to her cheeks was any indication, crimson probably covered her pale face in a blush. She squeaked when he lifted her with ease, laughing as she ungracefully tumbled into the basket. He glanced into the basket, his eyebrows raised in question.

"I'm okay." Chloe's answer came out more laugh than words as the pilot, Ted, helped her up.

Jake climbed into the basket with the grace of a panther and stalked toward her. "I'm sorry, Chloe. I didn't mean to toss you in like that."

He touched her arm, and heat spread from the contact. The man must be made of lava for how every touch raised her temperature faster than the giant furnace blowing above her. She smiled and placed her hand over his.

"No worries."

He glanced at her hand over his. She snatched it away and pretended to be very interested in the furnace firing above them. The basket lurched, sending her stomach into her throat. She couldn't wait to scratch this off her bucket list when they got back to the house.

She rushed to the side and leaned over the woven wall to look down as the balloon took off. Jake stepped up beside her, scanning the area. The whooshing feeling the ascent put in her stomach made her laugh. She tried to take everything in: the creek where it meandered past the field where they'd parked the vehicle, the bright white of the morning sun reflecting off of the snow, and the deep shadows still lingering in the bushes.

The darkness beneath a bush shifted, and her body froze. Had her stalker found them? Her heart pounded in her throat as she stared into the shadows, trying to discern what the movement belonged to. Jake peeked at her, then followed her gaze, stepping closer to her so their shoulders touched. A rabbit bounded out of the bush. She gasped, then dissolved into giggles. She needed to just relax. This whole stalker thing had her paranoid.

"Gosh, Jake, look at this view." She leaned against the basket and took it all in, glad she'd thought of hanging her camera around her neck before they took off.

The trees along the creek that weaved toward town had tiaras of sparkling snow on their black branches. The rainbow colors of the balloon reflected off the dark blue creek that snaked through snow-covered fields. She adjusted her settings for the light and snapped photo after photo.

"Are you ready for some real fun?" the pilot asked with an enormous smile.

"This isn't fun enough?" Chloe asked over her shoulder.

His smile widened as he shook his head. "Hang on."

The furnace blew loud above them in a steady stream of fire, and the balloon rocketed into the air. She squealed as her knees turned to jelly, and her stomach fell to her toes. This was absolutely amazing. She clung to the basket and laughed as the ascent slowed.

"Again!" she hollered at Ted and leaned on the wall.

Hanging her head out of the basket with her arms spread wide, the rush of the balloon rising had pure joy bubbling up and over her cup. She wobbled, and Jake's arm wrapped around her, anchoring her to the woven structure. With his strength holding her, she leaned out even farther, flying high like the sun.

The blasting of the furnace halted, and silence settled over them. When she straightened back into the basket, her head rested against Jake's shoulder. Wow, he'd had to get close. She could get used to this whole bodyguard thing.

She tilted her head back to look up at him, and something other than joy bubbled inside her. "Thanks for anchoring me."

Was her voice really that husky? She tried to calm her racing heart. With the way he stared down at her, she failed. He nodded, then stepped away. Chloe regretted the loss of his heat immediately.

She shook her head and turned to the pilot. "I think I've changed my mind."

"You ready to go down?" Concern laced the question.

"No. I don't think music is my future." She spun in a circle. "I want to be a hot-air balloon pilot when I grow up."

He tipped his head back and laughed. She turned back to the mountains jutting up from the valley with a sigh. She hoped Piper had gotten over her fear to enjoy this. To Chloe's way of thinking, this beat carnival rides hands down.

With the crisp air kissing her cheeks and the magnitude of creation spread before her, the hymn of flying away fell as a whisper from her lips. She'd sung that hymn a million times while lying in the hospital bed. It'd brought her comfort when the end looked near, a hope of a life in heaven with no sickness or pain. One day, she would fly away to glory, but she'd been blessed with a second chance at life. One she wouldn't waste. The hymn that had once seemed imminent now felt more a future promise. As the sun bathed her face in morning light, she closed her eyes and let the song soar out.

EIGHT

Jake scanned the restaurant again before sitting next to Chloe at the large table. The Back Door Grill had a great small-town vibe with money hanging on the walls and cheerful chatter filling the place to the corners. The thick aroma of fried food permeated the air and made Jake's mouth water. Relief eased his muscles when the greeter led them to the table in the corner. With how this place had tables crammed at all angles, it'd be hard to keep watch if they'd been seated in the middle.

"I can't tell you how glad I am that you could fill in at such short notice," Mr. Franklin, the festival's director, gushed at Chloe.

"I'm happy we didn't have something booked." Chloe twisted the menu in her hand. "Steamboat has been a wonderful diversion from the Texas winter. We don't have the beautiful snow and crisp air that really screams the season."

"We moved up from Louisiana about twenty years ago, so I know what you mean." The man chuckled as he opened his menu. "Nothing beats Colorado any season. Steamboat most of all."

This man reminded Jake of a captain they once had that promised the base in Afghanistan was the best out there. The sand trap ended up the worst base they'd ever had to launch from. Jake caught Rafe's eye and smirked. Rafe, for once, pressed his lips together and tucked his head to read the menu.

"What do you suggest, Mr. Franklin?" Piper asked as she scanned the menu.

"Everything here will get your mouth to watering. They make the best hamburgers in the state." The man wiped his hand across his mouth like he drooled at the mere thought of the food. He snagged the waitress as she passed their table. "Hun, do you think you can get us a Quadruple Bypass, Mac and Cheese Bites, and Tater Tatchos started before we order?"

Her shoulders slumped slightly, though she pasted on a smile. "Sure thing, Mr. Franklin, just as soon as I deliver this food."

Jake scanned the menu for the items the man had ordered. His eyes widened. Did the guy think he was feeding an army or what? He peeked over the menu at the plump man. Or maybe just himself.

Jake's lips pinched as he read the rest of the menu. There wasn't much here that Chloe could eat. He wondered if she could order the burgers without a bun. What must it be like to have a menu this big but only a few things safe to eat?

He leaned over to her where she scrutinized the menu. "Is there anything you can eat?"

Her smile didn't reach her eyes when she turned to him. "I'm going to have the chili."

"Is th—"

"Chloe, I've arranged for you to go to Ellie Smithton's house after we finish here." Mr. Franklin interrupted Jake, and Chloe leaned over and pointed to the little square with a GF in it next to the chili on the menu. "When her dad complained about the other artist dropping out to his family, that little girl begged until she was blue in the face for you to be the replacement."

"I'm excited to meet her." Chloe beamed across the table. "Hopefully, I can encourage her."

"I'm sure you can, darling." The man rubbed his hands together as the waitress approached for their orders. "That girl never leaves her house. It'll be good for her and her parents to see how you get on in the world, seeing as you have the same affliction and all. They just need to stop babying her and move on."

Chloe tensed as the obnoxious man turned to the waitress to order. Piper slammed her fist onto the table and looked hotter than a lizard in the desert. Jake understood the feeling as he clenched his hand on his leg. Chloe shook her head violently at her cousin and pointed her finger. Chloe pasted on a smile as the waitress turned to her.

"I'll have a bowl of chili, please."

"Mandy, sweetheart, make it extra special." Mr. Franklin rubbed the waitress on the arm.

She shifted away. "Sure thing, Mr. Franklin."

Mandy continued to take their orders. When she came to Jake, he hesitated. He'd never worried about what he would order before, but he saw the food in a different light.

"I'll take the chicken tacos." That seemed safe.

They all nodded politely as Mr. Franklin spouted on and on about nothing. He paused only to give lingering hugs to women patrons that walked by. When the appetizers arrived, Chloe shrank from the table now laden with wheat-covered food. Jake couldn't wait to get this meal done and over with. This man rivaled for the most arrogant man alive award.

When he didn't grab a plate and dig in like Rafe, Chloe leaned over to him. "You don't want any?"

"Nah." He shook his head and looked into her concerned eyes. "I'll wait until my meal gets here."

He didn't want to tell her he worried about getting her sick. The other night she'd said kissing a guy who'd drunk a beer could knock her out. He hadn't known what that meant, so he googled celiac. Not that he thought about kissing her. Well, thought about it much.

After reading several articles online, he had the fear of God thoroughly embedded into his soul. Was she so sensitive to gluten that even touching it could make her sick? What if he ate a deep-fried pickle, then needed to grab her hand to get her out of here? That minuscule contact could put some celiacs in bed for days. No, until this assignment finished, he'd stick with safe foods and not risk it.

Their meals arrived, and his eyes bulged at the size of their portions. Piper's bright green salad looked tempting piled high in the bowl. Rafe's and Mr. Franklin's sandwiches were both so thick Jake doubted they could get their mouths around them. He glanced at Chloe's chili as the waitress set it in front of her, and scowled. Chopped up mozzarella sticks covered the top.

Chloe put her hand on her neck and cleared her throat. "I'm really sorry. I guess I didn't read the menu right. I have celiac and can't eat the chili with these on top."

Mandy looked at the soup, then glared at Mr. Franklin.

Chloe continued, pulling the waitress's attention back. "I'll pay for this bowl, since I made a mistake, but is it possible to get a bowl without those on it?"

"It's not your fault, ma'am. I'll go get you another bowl right away." Mandy threw one last glare at Mr. Franklin, who gleefully stuffed his face, and rushed to the kitchen.

How could that fool be so insensitive? He'd even mentioned Chloe's celiac. Jake couldn't stand people like him, who had little regard for others.

"That looks good." Chloe's soft words drew his eyes to her. "I'm not sure how I missed that on the menu."

"You can eat these?" Jake studied his tacos.

She leaned in to scrutinize them. "They'd probably be okay. As long as the meat and tortillas weren't warmed on the same place the buns were."

"Do you want one?" Jake picked one up and extended it to her, glad he'd made a choice that wouldn't kill her.

Joy filled her eyes as she smiled. "No, thanks, but I'll take a bite."

Instead of taking the taco from him, she leaned close

and opened her mouth. He gulped as he moved the taco to her mouth. She took a bite, her lips skimming his fingertips. His heart took off like hummingbird wings.

She put her hand over her mouth and moaned. "That is so good."

"Do you want the rest?"

"Nah, chili's fine. But thanks for sharing." She lifted her smile to the waitress who placed a fresh bowl of chili on the table.

Jake tore his gaze away and focused on his own plate. He ripped a bite off of his taco, allowing the spicy flavor to jolt him back to reality. Just because Chloe attracted him like a bear to honey meant nothing. She was sweet and generous, nothing like how he pictured a celebrity to be.

It'd be plain stupid to let his attraction go further than that, though. She laughed at something Piper said, and the sound wove into his stomach and settled, just like her song had the day before. He creased his forehead and peeked at her. She'd been through just as much as he had and had come out the other side with joy. Could she be one who would understand his struggles, maybe be willing to come alongside him as he healed?

When the meal of torture finished, Chloe politely thanked Mr. Franklin for joining them for lunch. She had hardly eaten any of her meal, and Jake worried she felt sick. Piper pulled Chloe close as they left the restaurant, whispering in her ear. Good, they were easier to protect bunched together like hens. With Rafe guarding the rear, Jake rushed them outside to the vehicle.

The SUV doors had barely slammed shut before Rafe jumped into it. "Man, that guy was a grade A jerk."

"Oh no, he's passed the jerk level." Piper's voice seethed with anger.

Rafe twisted in his seat to look at her. "Pipster, I thought I was gonna have to wrap you around the waist and haul you off. You looked ready to pummel the man."

"It's a good thing I practice restraint." Piper punched her hand in her palm. "Otherwise, he'd be black and blue and not have use of those hands he likes to get all touchy-feely with."

Jake peeked in the rearview mirror at Chloe. She smiled but stared out the window. Did he need to take her to the hospital? He shouldn't have offered her a bite of his tacos. What if they made it on the griddle with the gluten products?

"Chloe, you hardly ate any of your chili. Are you feeling okay?" Jake's gaze connected with hers in the mirror.

Her cheeks turned pink as her eyes bounced to everyone in the car. "I'm fine. Chili just isn't one of my favorites. I had to eat a lot of it when I was in the hospital."

"Chili, broth, and plain, dry chicken." Piper pretended to gag. "We got so sick of those for a while neither of us could even look at them without wanting to vomit."

"Davis kept me updated when you got so sick. We both felt bad we weren't around to help when it got bad." Rafe rubbed his neck, his voice thick with regret.

"You two were doing more important things, like

playing hero to the world." Chloe leaned over and gave Piper a side hug. "Besides, I survived, and all because of this amazing woman who refused to leave my side for a minute. She even snuck me contraband."

"I wasn't going to let you go through that alone." Piper laughed. "Besides, it was the perfect opportunity to live out my fantasy of snagging a doctor."

Rafe turned in his seat, his forehead furrowed. "You fantasize about hooking up with a doctor?"

Piper's face turned bright red as she stared Rafe down. "Among other things."

Whoa, the tension zinging between those two had become tight. Davis would flip. Jake smiled, wondering if he should drop Davis an email and ruin Rafe's fun. He glanced at Rafe. Jake shook his head. Nah. Rafe knew the sister code.

Before the moment became any more awkward, Jake focused back on Chloe. "Do you want me to stop somewhere and grab you something to eat? There's a health food store close."

"How do you know that?" Her eyes lit with curiosity.

"Google."

Her smile widened, and Jake had to work to focus on the road and not her. "I'm fine, Jake. I have a stash of food in my purse if I get hungry."

Jake nodded, and his neck heated. He needed to worry about getting them to her fan's house safely, not whether or not Chloe would starve. His job description did not include dietician. He pulled into the driveway and scanned the street as he opened the door for Chloe. When he closed the door, she stepped up close to him and placed her hand on his arm. It tingled where she touched and raced to his shoulder, causing all his hair to stand on end.

"Thank you for worrying about me." She rose on her tiptoes and kissed his scarred cheek, the tingles multiplying by the power of a hundred.

A whoop on the other side of the vehicle had Jake pushing Chloe between him and the SUV. He needed to stay vigilant, not get distracted by pixies. Chloe's laughter behind him relaxed his muscles.

"Piper, you okay?" Chloe asked through her giggles.

"Yeah." Piper's wry reply caused Jake's mouth to twitch upward.

"Careful, it's slick." Rafe's voice held a tone Jake had never heard from his friend before.

Jake glanced to the other side of the vehicle, but the dark windows kept him from seeing anything. He placed his hand around Chloe's small waist and led her up the walk. They just needed to get inside, get the meet and greet over with, and escape to the safety of the house.

The squealing of a teenage girl broke into his thoughts with a jolt. A young woman stood at the house's door, her trembling hands covering her mouth as tears ran down her face. Chloe pulled out of Jake's arms and rushed up the walkway, wrapping her arms around the crying girl.

"I'm so glad to meet you, Ellie," Chloe said as Jake stepped up behind her.

"You have no idea what this means to me." Ellie sobbed into Chloe's shoulder.

"I think I have a pretty good idea." Chloe turned to Jake, her tears hanging on her lashes.

Jake's heart pinched, and he cleared his throat. "Why don't we go inside?"

The next four hours, Jake spent listening to more girl talk than he'd ever heard in his entire life. He found out more about Chloe's struggles with celiac as she encouraged Ellie. Chloe even talked the Smithtons into allowing her to hire her own celiac specialist to help Ellie.

Chloe hugged Ellie tight at the door as they left. "You have my number. Call or text me anytime. I'd love to hear from you."

Ellie nodded and sniffed. "Thanks, Chloe, for everything. Life doesn't seem like it will totally suck now."

Chloe's smile blinded him as Jake guided her by the elbow to the SUV. Man, she really blew his mind. She wrapped her arm around his and squeezed.

"That was the most amazing thing ever." Her cheery laugh made him smile.

"I bet that feels good, helping others like that." Jake wrapped his arm around her when they got to an icy patch.

"Imagine, using your weaknesses to help others get over theirs. Nothing beats that."

He looked down at her as her voice trailed off.

She trembled against him as she stared at the SUV. He followed her gaze, his gut hardening at the sight of a paper tucked between the wiper and windshield.

"Rafe," he barked out, pushing Chloe up against the house so he could search the vehicle.

With Rafe protecting the women, Jake methodically

checked every inch of the SUV. When he found nothing, he opened the back hatch and pulled out the Eyes Beyond invention June had provided them with. He didn't want to take any chances. As he scanned the vehicle for inconsistencies, plans ran through his mind. The need to get Chloe safe went beyond just doing his job, cementing into his very fiber. He pushed the thought aside, not willing to let the anxiety that image brought freeze him.

NINE

Chloe stood frozen against the house as Jake searched the vehicle. She tried not to think about what he might find, but the image of him blowing up from some kind of bomb kept her heart pounding viciously in her throat. The white paper waved in the wind, mocking the bravado she'd cloaked herself in.

Jake stomped up to where she huddled behind Rafe. "We're good."

His firm hand around her waist did little to lessen the fear lodged between her lungs. How had the creep found them? Dear Lord, what if he hurt Ellie?

She tried to turn back to the house. "The Smithtons."

"We'll take care of it." Jake tightened his grip, his face as hard as his tone.

After guiding her into the back seat, Jake snatched the note and slammed his door shut. He tossed the paper to Rafe and sped out of the neighborhood. Piper scooted to the middle seat and grabbed Chloe's shaking hands from her lap.

"What does it say?" Chloe hated how her voice trembled, how one person could affect her so much.

Rafe scanned the note. His jaw clenched, and he glanced over at Jake. That wasn't a good sign. Chloe's stomach twisted.

"Rafe?" Piper pushed.

Rafe cleared his throat and read. "'I've seen the way he holds you. Keep it up, and you'll regret it.'"

Chloe's eyes swung to Jake, who tightened his grip on the steering wheel. That made little sense. Sure, Jake had held her, but only to keep her from slipping. Was her stalker talking about how she'd kissed Jake's cheek earlier? Whoever this guy was, he'd upped the ante in this note.

"We're getting out of here." Jake's low tone sliced through the silence that had blanketed the vehicle's interior.

"Wait. I can't skip this concert." Chloe leaned forward, gripping her hand around Jake's seat.

"We can fly you back in for the concert, bring more protection with us, but we need to get you to the ranch where this guy can't get to you." Jake turned at the sign that pointed to the airport.

"What about all our stuff? I have appearances scheduled this week. All that information is at the house." Chloe's throat felt like it would close on her.

"Chlo, this guy isn't playing games." Rafe turned in the seat.

"What if I go back to the house and gather up our stuff?" Piper's soft voice turned everyone's attention to her. "I can start calling our contacts and figuring out what we can do virtually from the ranch."

Chloe shook her head as her anxiety built. "Piper, no—"

"Listen. It makes sense. I'm your manager. It's my job to take care of things." Piper hugged her close. "Rafe and I will gather everything up here, then drive down to this ranch of theirs."

"But what if he follows you guys, or what if he gets mad and hurts you?"

"Don't worry. We'll be quick, and Rafe will keep me safe." Piper gazed at Rafe.

Rafe swallowed as he nodded. "Always."

Chloe should've been celebrating the look that passed between her two friends, but the terror of the moment squashed any delightful feelings. She didn't know what to do. Leaving Piper behind didn't seem right. She pulled her bottom lip between her teeth and bit so hard she winced.

Rafe placed his hand on her knee. "Chloe, this will work. I can spot a tail a mile away. We'll take back roads and be to the ranch later tonight." He squeezed her knee. "I won't let anything happen to our Piper, I promise."

Jake pulled his phone out and dialed. "Yes, I need to schedule an emergency flight at the earliest available time, please."

His tense voice dumped ice down her back. How was this happening? She wasn't anyone special. Hadn't even really made it yet. She stared out the window as Steamboat whizzed by. Clouds darkened the sky over the mountains like how terror turned the perfect day to gloom.

Jake tossed his phone into the cup holder. "The next hour is wide open. We can taxi as soon as I get everything checked. Rafe, you and Piper will want to get out of here quick. There's a storm blowing in."

"Is it safe to fly?" Chloe eyed the menacing clouds again, wishing they could go back to the house and bunker down.

"It'll probably be a bumpier ride than normal, but it should be all right." Jake confidently glanced in the rearview mirror at her. "Chloe, I've been flying since I was fourteen. We'll be fine, I promise."

She nodded and took a fortifying breath. Just because panic pounded in her chest, didn't mean she had to give in to it. Hadn't she learned that with all she'd been through. Jake stopped next to a tiny, sleek airplane that looked like little more than a tin can. Her palms turned slick with sweat.

"Wait in here while I get the plane prepped." Jake didn't pause for an answer.

A gust of frigid air blew into the vehicle before the door slammed. Chloe shivered and pulled out her phone. She wanted to call and talk to the band herself.

"Chloe! How's the starlet doing today?" Chet's friendly voice answered.

While he'd just joined the band three months before when her other guitarist got a better gig, he had great vision. She'd enjoyed working on new songs with him.

"Hey, Chet. We have a bit of an issue."

"You didn't crash your computer again, did you?"

Of course he had to bring up the time she'd destroyed her computer and lost all the songs they'd been working on.

"No, nothing like that." She cleared her throat, embarrassed by the entire situation. "I'm having some issues with a guy. He started leaving messages on the phone back home. Anyway, he followed us here."

"Really? Are you okay?"

"Yeah, but the messages have escalated. I'm flying out in a few minutes with my security. Piper will be driving down with our stuff and a friend."

"Wow, what about the concert?"

"The security firm is based out of Glenwood Springs, so we'll fly up on Friday for practice and the concert. I know it's not ideal, but ..."

"No, your safety is the most important thing." His voice sounded tight. "You said Piper's leaving, too?"

Chloe cringed. The poor guy had a little crush on Piper, had even gotten up the nerve to ask her on a date. He wasn't Piper's type. Only one man had ever filled that description. Chloe peeked at Rafe, who talked in low tones on his phone.

"Yeah, I have some interviews and stuff she's going to try to coordinate from Glenwood. Plus, her brother would flip if we left her here alone."

Piper elbowed Chloe in the side and stuck out her tongue.

"Oh, okay." Chet's dejected voice made Chloe feel sorry for him, but Piper had been honest with him from the start.

Chloe wanted off the phone. "Listen, Chet, I gotta go.

Could you let the others know that we'll call later to work out Friday?"

"Sure thing. Keep safe."

Chloe tapped the end icon and smiled at Piper. "It seems your admirer is upset you're leaving town."

Piper groaned and rolled her eyes. "I feel bad. Maybe I should've said yes."

"What's this?" Rafe turned in the seat and looked between the two of them.

Chloe stifled a smile as a plan formed. "My guitarist, Chet, has been wanting Piper to go out to dinner. She's sparked his fancy, some would say."

"You told him no?" Rafe's eyes narrowed at Piper.

"Yeah, but I keep wondering if I should go ahead and go. We've spent a fair amount of time with him lately, working on songs and such." Piper shrugged. "He's nice."

"But you're not attracted to him?" Rafe asked.

"It's not that." Piper rubbed her collar as her cheeks pinked.

"So, you are attracted?" he pushed.

"He's hot." Chloe smiled and nudged Piper. "Smoking hot."

Rafe's muscles tightened. "Why not go out with him then?"

Piper's cheeks turned bright red. "Because, I'm not going to get attached to someone who will realize sooner rather than later that he'd rather date someone else, especially with the amount of gorgeous groupies always storming him at the shows."

Chloe's heart sank. She should've kept her big mouth shut.

Rafe growled low. "What is that supposed to mean?"

Piper crossed her arms. "I'm done talking about this."

"Piper." Rafe pursed his lips together.

Thankfully, Jake opened Chloe's door at that moment, cutting off the awkward conversation. Jake had pulled winter gear over his clothes, making Chloe wonder if the plane had heaters.

He lifted snow pants to her. "These will be big, but why don't you pull them on."

She nodded and worked to get into them while Piper got out of the vehicle. Rafe flinched when the door slammed. He flexed his fingers, then turned to Chloe.

"Does she like this guy?" His voice sounded strained.

"He's nice, always seeks her out and jokes with her." Chloe paused when Rafe glanced at Piper out the back window where she leaned against the SUV. His jaw clenched.

Should Chloe push this? Piper would kill her. But then again, Piper would never believe in herself enough to see Rafe's attraction.

Chloe prayed Piper would forgive her. "I think she should go for it, personally. Chet sees what a beautiful person she is on the inside and out." Her words snapped Rafe's eyes to her. "But she's still hung up on her first love. Too bad the idiot never saw her as anything but his friend's little sister."

Chloe gave Rafe a pointed look before stepping out the door. She reached in for her purse. It was adorable how Rafe sat blinking like he couldn't process what she'd just told him. He'd always been a smart kid. He could figure it out.

"But—" He was cut off by Jake.

"We need to go." Jake stalked to the SUV.

Dread washed through Chloe as she straightened from the doorway.

Piper threw her arms around Chloe's neck. "I'll see you soon."

"Don't you think you should come with?" Chloe's throat didn't seem to want to work.

"No, I need that information from the house." Piper squeezed Chloe and stepped back. "Besides, we'll be right behind you. I say ice cream and chick flicks tonight."

Chloe laughed. "That sounds perfect."

Chloe gave Piper one last hug and followed Jake to the front passenger door of the plane. He helped her climb into the seat next to the pilot's and shut the door with a snap. She turned and surveyed the interior. The sparse cabin was little more than a coffin with wings. The back had four seats facing each other in rows of two. They'd strapped gear behind the back two seats with a criss-crossing cargo net. The smooth walls curved up in a cylinder, making Chloe feel like they were closing in on her. She wiggled her numb fingers and clenched her hands together.

Jake climbed in on the pilot's side and gave her a tight smile. "Ready?"

"No."

His smile broadened, and he clicked buttons and knobs. He pointed to the headset hung next to her as he talked to air traffic control. She nodded and took one last look at Piper. She stood with her arms tight against her. Her teeth worried her thumb nail. Chloe forced a smile and waved out the window. Piper's shoulders curved forward as she returned the wave. Would Chloe ever stop causing her cousin pain?

Rafe put his arm around Piper, waved at the plane, then led her around the SUV. Chloe held her breath as Piper grabbed his arm when he tried to get her in the vehicle and asked him something. His expression softened. He lifted his hand and tucked a piece of stray hair behind her ear, leaning closer as he replied. She nodded, and he kissed her on the forehead before guiding her into the SUV. Chloe sighed with happiness. Maybe something good would come out of this mess.

She shook her head and reached for the headset. Laughter bubbled out as she wondered what the large earphones looked like extending miles past her tiny head. She turned to Jake and made a face.

"They're a little big for you." Jake's voice coming out of the headset made her jump.

His laugh slid down her spine and settled in her toes. Jake in concentrated form caused all kinds of jumblies in her insides. She might just keep these on forever.

Jake drove the plane toward the runway. Every bump bounced her stomach into her throat. She gripped the door in a death grip.

"We'd like to thank you for choosing to fly Stryker Airlines today." Jake's voice had a cheery tone that pulled her attention to him. "Please be sure your seat is in the upright position and that your tray table is up."

He peeked over at her and winked. His joking relaxed her. Where had that sense of humor been the last few days?

"Will snacks be passed out? I could use a ginger ale." Chloe wrapped her hands around her seatbelt to keep them from clenching.

"All I have is water, ma'am. But you'll have to fly so I can get it."

"I think I'll live."

"Chloe, this isn't going to be the smoothest flight you've ever had." Jake reached over her and pointed to the door. "There are bags in the door if you get sick."

"Okay." The thought of her chili lunch making a second appearance made her cringe.

"I'm going to try to skirt the storm, but it's moving in fast. Thankfully, it's a quick flight, only about thirty minutes."

Maybe they all should've just driven. Jake squared up with the runway and throttled up. She tightened her hands on the belt, willing her eyes to stay open. The plane lifted into the air and swooped as a gust of wind hit the wing. Jake pointed the plane south over the mountains. The higher they climbed, the colder it got. She'd have been a Popsicle if Jake hadn't made her put on the snow pants. The plane dipped, and Chloe stifled a gasp.

"So you've been flying since you were fourteen?" If she didn't get him talking, she'd lose it.

"My dad taught me in his Cub."

"Cub?"

"It's a smaller plane, only a two seater."

"Is it always this cold in these small planes?" Chloe pulled her hands into her coat, wishing she had worried more about the weather and not how cute she looked when they had left the house that morning.

Jake's eyebrows furrowed before he reached back and plopped a pack in her lap. "There should be gloves and a hat in there. It can be colder in these small planes, though usually not this cold. The temp is plummeting too fast for the plane to compensate."

The plane jerked again, and Chloe almost dropped the glove she had found. Jake's hands gripped on the steering mechanism. His lips flattened as he flipped some switches and checked gauges.

"Everything all right?" She wished she knew something about flying, though maybe it was a blessing she didn't.

"Yeah, it'll be okay. See how the windshield is frosting?" He pointed to the bottom of the windshield where ice crept up like every ice princess movie ever made.

She swallowed and nodded. "Yeah."

"The moisture from the storm and the falling temperature isn't working in our favor right now."

"Should we turn back?"

He paused, his cheek muscle ticking, before he shook his head. "We're almost halfway there. I'm going to adjust our flight path east a little to try to put some distance between us and the head of the storm."

The plane dropped from turbulence, and a squeak snuck out of her. She swallowed the fear and chili in her throat. Her stomach twisted as the ice spider-webbed farther up the windshield. She leaned forward, her eyes squinting as something black glided from the nose of the plane back, marring the pristine white paint.

"Jake, is that supposed to happen?" She pointed at the liquid and watched his reaction.

His eyes widened and nostrils flared before quickly masking to neutral. "Chloe, start looking for a place to land. We have to put this down."

Land? As in crash? She gulped down her breaths to stay quiet. They both scanned outside the windows. She cursed her short height, wishing she could get a higher angle to see more. Her body shook as her gaze landed on the insidious white clouds that rolled over the mountain like billowing waves of smoke.

"Mayday, 6A-32 Cherokee 6 going down." Jake's clipped words froze her gut.

As he relayed their information, Chloe frantically scanned the terrain, not really knowing what to look for. She worried her attempt to stay calm and collected failed miserably. A smooth area between mountains looked open enough to land. She squinted as the outline of a cabin tucked in the woods beyond the opening came into view.

"Jake." She pointed to the area.

Jake stretched in his seat, scrutinizing the terrain. "Perfect, Chloe. Hold on. This will be rough."

She clenched every muscle in her body and prayed like her life depended on it—which it probably did. The plane veered as a gust of wind pushed them off course. Chloe's eyes opened wide as saucers as she pinged her gaze out the window and back to Jake. Jake grimaced, the strain in his muscles cording his neck as he fought against the weather.

They lowered closer and closer to the ground. She wanted to squeeze her eyes tight, but fear kept them glued open. She clamped her teeth together as the plane bounced off the ground. If she died, at least it wasn't stuck in a hospital bed.

The plane bounced again, and she gripped her seat-belt to keep from grabbing the steering handles in front of her. They skidded across the snow, heading straight for a jumble of boulders. Maybe she hadn't picked a perfect place after all. She slammed her eyes closed, no longer able to watch the end of her life unfold.

Her heart thudded in her chest as the plane slammed to a stop and jerked her forward. She froze. Nothing but her choppy breaths and the gusting wind assaulting the outside of the plane hit her ears. She sucked in air and held it, waiting for the inevitable explosion like the movies always showed. She flinched when Jake's hand slid along her neck and eased behind her head.

"Chloe, are you all right?"

No, she wasn't. She couldn't breathe. The air had bottled up in her chest, and though she panted, she felt like she couldn't get enough. She shook her head, her hands fumbling with the buckle—needing to get out.

Chloe snapped her eyes open to her hands, not wanting to see Jake's disappointment in her spiral out of control. A sob tore from her chest, and she quickly swallowed the next one. Why wouldn't this stupid buckle work?

She heard a clicking sound, then Jake's hands covered hers. "Chloe, it's okay. We'll be okay."

As he unbuckled her belt, she chanced a glance over at him. He'd turned in his seat, angling his legs toward her. He glanced outside, his demeanor unflustered, calming her as he clicked the buckle free.

She tore the straps over her head and threw herself into Jake. She didn't care if it made her desperate, but she needed him to hold her, even if only for a minute. For once, her petite form came in handy as she climbed into his lap and buried her face in his neck.

The scent of sweat and fear rose from his skin, but with it the soothing scent of pine and citrus. If they'd survived the crash, they could survive the wait for help, especially with Jake here. He hugged her tightly against him. His presence bound all her fears that threatened to tear her to pieces—holding her together.

TEN

Jake's nerves threatened to shred apart and whip away in the wind. He wrapped his arms tighter around Chloe, though the yoke of the plane dug into his side and his leg cramped from the awkward position. They needed to get moving, to get everything they could from the plane to the cabin nestled in the trees before the storm hit. Still, he held her, needing to take a minute to thank God they'd survived and pray that Jake could maintain that status until someone found them.

"Chloe, we need to get the gear and make our way to that cabin." He skirted his fingers along her neck, wishing he had a scarf or coat with a hood.

She nodded and pulled back, a tear hanging on her thick eyelashes. "You were amazing. You landed so softly, like the ground was a pillow." She blinked, and the tear tracked down her cheek.

He rubbed his thumb along her soft skin, catching the drop before it fell. "I should've known better. That front was colder than I expected." He trailed his thumb along her jaw. "Now, you ...you were the amazing one. Our landing would've been a lot worse if you hadn't seen this open valley. You're not hurt, are you?"

She closed her eyes and leaned into his hand. "No. What happened? What was that black stuff?"

"Oil. The air tube must've frozen over. The lack of air broke the seal. If you hadn't found this place to land, the engine would've seized."

He swallowed down the urge to kiss her and cleared his throat. "Can you crawl back and start unbuckling the cargo straps from the hold? We'll want to take as much as we can now, before that storm hits. I'm not sure how many trips, if any, I can make before the snow starts really coming down."

She nodded and loosened her arms from around his neck. Before she turned to climb to the back of the plane's cabin, she glanced at him. She opened her mouth, then closed it with a huff. Her face morphed from uncertainty to determination with the set of her delicate jaw and a curt nod. She slid her fingers through his beard and pressed her lips to his in a soft, testing stroke.

Electricity sparked where her mouth touched his, and he fisted his hands in her coat to keep himself grounded. She pulled away far too quickly for his liking. Could she feel his pulse hammering against her fingertips as she traced them along his neck?

She stared at his lips, increasing his heart beat even more, then lifted her eyes to his. "Thank you, Jake."

He nodded, not sure what she was thanking him for. For crashing the plane? How about that he got them stranded with a winter storm blowing in? The thought galvanized him to get moving.

"Let's get going." His voice tumbled out like boulders down a mountain.

Her cheeks pinked, but she nodded and climbed over the seats to the back. He couldn't worry right now if he embarrassed her or not. He needed to call in their location and get them to the cabin.

With the radio call put in to ATC, Jake pushed open his door and surveyed the ground. The plane had landed flat on its belly with its nose less than a foot from a jumble of rocks. The clouds rolled fast over the mountain ridge, heading toward them. They needed to get everything they could in one trip. He doubted they'd be able to make another.

He stepped out, sank to his hips in the soft snow, and groaned. He hoped the snowshoes were still in the cargo hold. Trudging his way to the back door, he panted hard while he opened it.

"Chloe, hand me that cargo net."

She'd taken off his huge gloves to work. Her fingers shook and were red as she handed him the net. He nodded to her and laid the net out on top of the snow.

"Start passing me packs." Jake pointed to the outdoor packs full of emergency supplies.

She grabbed the first one and grunted when she couldn't lift it. She leveraged her legs against the seats and dragged the pack to Jake. He lifted it and plopped it in the middle of the net. He'd probably only be able to haul four of the heavy things at a time.

"While you're digging through that stuff, see if there

are snowshoes back there." Jake cringed as Chloe slipped and banged hard against the seat. "You okay?"

"I'm fine." Her face reddened as she dragged a third pack over.

After the fourth pack was in the middle of the net, Jake began weaving and tying ends together so he could pull the bundle. He turned back to the plane to find Chloe's feet sticking out of the hold. With a whoop, she backed out and held up two pairs of snowshoes in triumph.

He sighed, his chest expanding with relief. "Awesome. Those will make this easier."

She disappeared back into the hold and came out with a backboard. "Could we use this as a sled?"

Warmth spread out to his fingers. He liked how she thought, trying to look at what they had and how to make it help. She hadn't whined once, just dug in and pushed through the pain. Even during the crash, she hadn't screamed or freaked out.

He smiled widely at her. "That's a brilliant idea."

Her eyes sparkled as she handed it to him. He positioned the heavy load on the backboard and strapped them together the best he could. He leaned on the load and caught his breath.

When he turned back to the plane, Chloe had grabbed her purse from the seat and a smaller pack from the back. She sat, trying to put on the snowshoes. He climbed into the plane and knocked the snow off his boots.

After strapping on the snowshoes, he made sure Chloe's were tight. He gazed out the open door at the long trek to the cabin and prayed for sustained strength. This might be one of the hardest quarter-mile walks he'd ever taken.

"Ready?" Jake asked.

She nodded. She looked so petite with his large gloves she'd pulled back on and the pack hanging from her back. Would he be able to keep her safe? He shook off the troubling thought and stepped out of the door. Doubt had no room in his brain right now.

"This snow is deep. Might be taller than you, which wouldn't take much," he said as he helped her out.

She softly elbowed him in the gut. "Be nice."

"It'll be easier if you follow me, that way you have a bit of a trail." Jake closed the door to the plane and slung on his backpack.

"Shouldn't I break a trail for you?" Chloe put her hand up to block the wind.

"Honey, you're so light, I doubt you even need the snowshoes." He moved to the straps of the makeshift sled. "Besides, I want to go in front just in case there's a hidden trench or something."

"Okay." Her voice shook, but he ignored it.

He looped the sled strap over his body and pulled. His feet sank into the ground, but the sled didn't move. He planted his feet and pulled again, praying his prosthetic stayed where it was supposed to. If he could just get the sled moving, he could drag it all the way. Chloe grunted behind him, and the sled slid toward him. He scrambled to get his feet on top of the snow and keep the mass moving.

The strap dug into his chest as he strained against the

weight. Little by little, they moved toward the cabin. The wind howled down the mountain and pelted them with stinging ice. He ran through what he'd need to do repeatedly in his head like a mantra. They couldn't reach the cabin fast enough. Wood, fire, more wood, water, food, more wood.

A squeak had him turning as he pulled.

"I'm fine. Keep going," Chloe called before he could look back.

She'd stayed right behind him, pushing the sled when it got stuck. Her grunts and gasps floated to him on the wind, but never once had a complaint left her mouth.

When they were a hundred yards from the cabin, and the snow blew so heavy Jake could hardly see, he unstrapped the net and shouldered the first pack. He could make it faster if he carried them one at a time. He needed to get Chloe inside now, before the storm got worse.

"Come on." He motioned her around the sled, then took off for the cabin.

Her labored breathing kept up with him the entire way. He pushed open the sagging door, tossed his packs into the corner, and turned back for the rest of the gear without even surveying the cabin. Two more trips and everything sat lined along the wall of the one-room cabin. Chloe had swept out the stone fireplace and built a fire with the wood that someone had left.

"I think something is stuck in the chimney. The smoke isn't going up." Chloe leaned into the fireplace and looked up.

"On it." Jake headed back outside, grabbing the hatchet Chloe had found in one of the packs.

He needed to work fast if he wanted to gather enough wood before the storm closed in around them. He found the closest sapling, chopped it down, then trekked back to the cabin. He hefted himself onto the cabin roof and prayed the thing didn't collapse.

When he got to the chimney, he leaned over it and hollered down, "Chloe, get out of the way."

Taking the thick end of the sapling, he rammed it down the hole until whatever blocked the opening broke free. He tossed the sapling off the roof in front of the door and made his way down. He'd drag that inside, just in case they needed it again. Since Chloe already had a fire going, wood moved up on the importance list.

He hacked three dead trees down and dragged them to the front of the cabin. Then, he chopped the trees into five-foot sections and loaded them into the cabin. Chloe had a fire roaring and had found a camp pot she'd set with water near the flames.

The cabin was warm and sparse, barely a twelve-foot square, but that didn't bother Jake. It would make the space easy to heat. It was old and sagging in one corner, making the door hard to open and close. There were no windows he had to worry about, and with him climbing up on the roof, at least part of it was sturdy. He'd check the rest more closely after he finished his list of things to do. He couldn't ask for a better place to be stranded in, though, with it tucked into the trees for protection.

"You all right?" Jake panted out the question.

She nodded, though worry lingered in her eyes.

"I'm going to try to get one more load of firewood."

"Okay."

He turned back out and stomped into the forest. He only got two more trees before the snow swirled so thick he worried he wouldn't find the cabin if he waited anymore. He'd heard those stories of people dying in a blizzard two feet from safety, simply because they couldn't find it. He wasn't about to be one of them. He had a pixie to keep safe.

He stacked the last of the wood up against the wall and frowned. It wasn't a lot, but hopefully, it'd be enough to make it through the storm. Then, he would get more.

"Jake, come and warm up." Chloe pulled him toward the fire.

He scanned the cabin, wondering what else needed done. Exhaustion weighed his limbs down. He'd been through the grueling training for the Special Ops team and missions that had taken everything out of him. He knew if he sat, he wouldn't be able to get back up.

"Come on." Chloe tugged his arm again. "We have a mountain of wood, food, water, and medical supplies. There's nothing that can't wait to be done. I'm exhausted, so I can't imagine how you feel. You did ten times as much work as I did."

He stared at how the soft light from the fire danced shadows across her face. He lifted his hand and pushed his gloved fingers through her short, curly hair that stuck in all directions from sweat. His ears rang with the rushing of his blood, and the storm that rattled the cabin seemed distant. She was right. He needed to rest.

He tore off his gloves with his teeth. She took them

from him and hung them from the cargo net she'd somehow hung along the wall. Her wet gear dried on hooks she'd fashioned along the netting. She'd been just as busy as he had.

His fingers fumbled with his zipper, and he huffed at their inability to function. She pushed his hands away and unzipped his coat. He should help her, but his muscles refused to move. She reached for his collar, lifting on her toes and kissing his jaw.

He grabbed onto her belt loop and stared down at her. His heart thundered in his chest, making him wonder if he was as tired as he thought. He gave a little tug, and she stepped closer.

He lowered his head and muttered, "You're so beautiful."

He kissed her soft lips that tasted of sugared coffee. She must've found the MREs. He tasted her again, wondering if a man could live off kisses alone. Doubtful. But, man, what a way to go. She ran her hands up his neck and into his hair with a sigh. He deepened the kiss, his hand skimming along the skin of her back that her arms, wrapped around his neck, exposed.

She yelped and grinned against his mouth. "Cold fingers." She kissed him one more time and took her hands from his hair. "Come on, hero." She slid his coat from his shoulders. "Let's get you warmed and something to drink."

He leaned down and kissed below her ear. "I'm not cold anymore," he whispered against her neck.

"Jake."

A gust of wind rattled the house. She jumped away

from him and grabbed his coat from where she'd dropped it on the floor. The cold and fatigue from earlier sank back into his bones.

She wagged her finger at him with a stern look on her face that her smile ruined. "Go sit."

She pointed to the fire where a mug still steamed on the floor next to a sleeping bag. He stepped out of his wet snow pants, handed them to her, then sank to the floor. As he drank the hot coffee, he tried to think of what he'd need to do next. His thoughts could only focus on the flicking flames that danced before him and the need to keep Chloe safe, no matter the cost.

ELEVEN

Chloe rummaged through the packs, trying to be as quiet as possible, though with the way the storm raged against the cabin, she could probably bang drums and it wouldn't make a difference. She glanced at Jake, her heart picking up at the sight of him. Or it could be the memory of his scorching kiss that had her heart racing. She hadn't needed the fire so badly after that.

She fanned her face with her hands and got back to work. She'd worried when he took so long to get firewood and the storm's assault had increased. She'd almost gone and looked for him when he came in half dead on his feet. Just dragging the four hundred-pound packs through the snow should have zapped his energy, but then he chopped down half the forest. She shook her head. And the Army said they couldn't use him? They were idiots.

The cabin groaned against a gust of wind that blew through the cracks in the logs and made her shudder. She stilled her hands and stared at the roof, waiting for it to collapse on her. As glad as she was to not be stuck out in the plane, she wondered if the cabin would finally return to nature with them in it.

The cabin settled into a normal creaking, and Chloe went back to organizing the supplies. She really should lie down and rest. She felt as if her arms would fall off at any minute. Yet she had to know if her suspicions were right.

She laid the last of the supplies out in their respective piles and ran her fingers between her eyes to relieve her building headache. These guys took their survival seriously. Each pack had enough dehydrated meals for three days, a firestarter, some kind of mug that doubled as a cooking pot, a sleeping bag, extra clothes, and a folding multitask tool.

They had enough to comfortably stay alive for a while, like some kind of intense camping trip—that was if one of them didn't have celiac. As she'd unpacked the first bag, she had a sinking feeling in her gut. The MREs all contained gluten. Jake had come through the door at that moment, lugging a large load of wood, his face creased with fatigue. She'd tried to play it cool and not show her inner freak out.

Jake not noticing probably had to do with his intense focus on wood and the fact that he ran on fumes. Even then, he'd paused and asked if she was okay. How much of his push came from protecting her? If he was alone, he probably could've survived with a lot less.

After he went back outside for more wood, she'd made three piles of food: a glutinous gluttony pile, a stack safe for her to eat, and a third one that she could eat if she absolutely had to. The measly pile of food without gluten had her praying they'd be found quickly. While the third pile had MREs that weren't full of blatant gluten like the pasta meals, the preservatives hid the poison. The question would be how much could her body ingest before it revolted? With her supplements that helped block the gluten back at the house, her supply she kept in her purse would only last four days max. Thank God she'd gotten used to carrying food in her large purse.

She weaved, her tired body finally calling it quits. She tiptoed to the fire, set another log on, then crawled into the second sleeping bag she'd laid out near the warmth. She stared into the flames as they flicked and swayed against the rock chimney.

Surely someone would find them as soon as the weather cleared. Her stomach growled, and she curled in on herself. She probably should have eaten her chili instead of being so picky. She'd eaten one of her meal bars. It hadn't made a dent in her hunger, but it would have to do.

Tears stung her nose. She rolled her eyes in disgust and flopped on to her back. She couldn't get all weepy now. It wouldn't help the situation any. Tears never had made a difference in her circumstances, so she'd determined soon after her diagnosis to keep them firmly in her head where they belonged. The stupid airplane crash had shaken them loose.

She turned her head to Jake. He had conked out on the sleeping bag the instant he'd lain down. *You're so beautiful.* Did he really think so, or was that the exhaustion talking?

She definitely wasn't up to par on her appearance this evening. She could only imagine how crazy her hair must stick up in all directions, with her sweating like a pig on the hike over to the cabin and the stocking cap keeping all that nastiness in.

Still, the words had slid like hot fudge over ice cream into the frigid depths of her soul—that place where she'd buried her dreams of happily ever after. Jake didn't seem the type to just throw words out there with his quiet demeanor and serious attitude. She'd never felt comfort like she did when he was near.

Comfort wasn't really the right word. She felt that when she curled up under her favorite blanket to read a book. More like serenity. She traced his profile with her eyes. His arm cradled his head in a pillow. She hardly noticed his scar anymore where it slashed across his cheek bone through his beard. She had been tempted to take off his prosthetic so he'd be more comfortable but hadn't had the nerve to. Would he ever let down his guard enough to show her? Could she let down hers to reveal all her vulnerable bits she hid beneath the perky musician?

She closed her eyes against the tears that blurred her vision. She wanted to. Needed to share what hid behind the brave front. Not that she wanted to go all weepy and weak on him, but having someone who'd gone through hell and back to lean on would be nice too.

She opened her eyes. There was only one way to find out. With a set of her jaw and a fluttering in her chest, she scooted her sleeping bag over to Jake's side. She filled her lungs with air and held it as she laid her head on his chest.

Jake's muscles tensed. She squeezed her eyes shut, waiting for him to push her away. His body relaxed with his exhale, and she copied the motion.

"Chloe?" His voice sounded groggy.

She tilted her face up, needing to see his reaction. "I ... Can I lay with you? I guess I'm a little scared right now, and ... you calm me."

His eyebrows rose before he schooled them. He wet his lips, his Adam's apple moving in a hard, obvious swallow. Slowly, he nodded, and relief rushed through her in a swoop that left her lightheaded.

"Okay." His voice was soft.

She'd take it. Chloe wrapped her arm around his chest and snuggled in closer. She closed her eyes and the worries racing through her head slowed. With a sigh, she relaxed even more into him.

When Jake's arm wound around her back and his other hand traced lazily up and down her arm, Chloe smiled as exhaustion finally dragged her toward sleep. Just before she nodded off, Jake's whisper about taking care of her followed her into her dreams.

TWELVE

Jake woke with a start and froze to assess the weight pinning his chest to the floor. The weight shifted, and he remembered falling asleep holding Chloe. He eased as recognition of her arm gripped in his and her faint snore hit him.

He relaxed back onto the floor, surprised at how hard he'd slept. Even more astonishing was the fact that he hadn't woken up screaming in terror and ready to fight. Did he have intense exhaustion to thank for that or the gorgeous woman whose words bolstered his heart?

He shifted his legs and cringed as pain shot up his knee and into his thigh. He probably should have taken off his prosthetic. An ache built in the back of his throat. Would Chloe still want to snuggle up to him when she saw his stump? It was easy to forget he wasn't whole when his pants covered the evidence. She didn't seem like the type to run scared from his injury, but he'd seen enough heartbreak in the military hospital and rehab to know some couldn't take reality.

The storm continued its onslaught against the cabin with wind howling like an F-16 buzzing the tower. He needed to get up, stoke the fire, and check to make sure they hadn't gotten snowed in. Chloe shifted, making a mewing noise almost like a kitten, then wrapped her hand over his shoulder. She nuzzled her nose into his neck, her soft breath raising his hair to stand at attention. He could get used to waking up like this every morning.

As much as he didn't want this moment to end—ever—he needed to check things. If he wanted the possibility of waking up with Chloe in his arms every morning for years to come, he had to keep them alive. His brain stumbled over that thought, and heat spread through his chest, amazed at the truth of the statement. Everything he'd ever hoped for in a wife had been bundled up in the pixie in his arms. He'd be an idiot to not at least consider seeing where this could go.

He shifted to the side, trying to slide away without waking her up. She tensed, then threaded her fingers through his hair. Tingles spread from his scalp down his neck.

"Jake?" Her deep husky voice had him debating getting up after all.

His voice caught on the lump stuck in his throat and came out little more than a whisper. "I need to check things."

She huffed, and her shoulders rose and fell like Eva's did when she pouted. She moved her face closer and pressed a lingering kiss to his neck. The tingles fired to a million bottle rockets and shot straight to his toes. Maybe the fire could wait. He glanced at the small lump in the fireplace. He growled. Nope, duty called.

He rolled onto his side, easing her onto her back, and propped himself on his elbow. With only embers glowing, he could barely see Chloe's face in the dark. The light reflected off of her wide eyes looking up at him. He ran the back of his fingers along her soft cheek. It was such a contrast to his rough fingers.

She inhaled sharply and held her breath. What would it be like to wake up every morning with her? He rubbed his thumb on her neck in the place where she'd kissed him. Her pulse beat wildly against his skin. His mouth turned up on one side, knowing he caused just as much of an increase in her heart rate as she did to his.

He bent down and kissed where her pulse thumped against her neck. "Good morning, Chloe," he whispered and kissed her below the ear.

He sat up before she distracted him any longer and stifled the moan of pain that threatened to ruin his image. Man, he hurt. Chloe grumbled low. Jake peeked at her. She'd thrown her arm over her eyes and her lips were turned down in a pout.

"You sure know how to wake a girl up," Chloe muttered. "And they call women teases."

Jake chuckled under his breath. He definitely had to get them through this because she was just too much fun to be around. He couldn't resist her challenge and leaned down, brushing his lips softly against hers. When he backed away, she pulled him to her and kissed him deeply. The roar of the wind, the low burn of the embers, and the deep-seated fear that he'd fail her disappeared until all that existed was her and him.

Her stomach growled loudly, causing her to laugh against his lips. "Well, that's embarrassing."

He spread his hand over her flat stomach and kissed her softly one more time. "Right. Fire. Food."

She'd reduced his brain to one and two-syllable words like a caveman. He pulled himself away with a groan, half out of regret for leaving their little make-out session but mostly out of pain. Hopefully, she thought the former caused the groan rather than the latter. Though, by the way he limped to the firewood, he doubted he fooled her.

He focused on getting the fire back up, not looking at her until he finished the job. He didn't think he could stay away from the temptation of returning for more kisses. When a good flame burned and a camp pot they'd filled with snow the night before sat close to the fire to boil for coffee, he turned to get some food.

Chloe sat crossed-legged in her sleeping bag like a bird in a nest. She fingered the tie strap, her bottom lip worried between her teeth. Was she still scared they wouldn't be found?

"Fire's done. Now, to food." He rubbed his hands together and smiled at her in encouragement.

"Yeah, about that." Chloe cringed and rubbed her fingers up her forehead as her eyes scrunched closed. "Do you happen to know how long this storm is supposed to last?"

He scratched at his beard as unease set in. "The forecast said two or three days."

She glanced toward the ceiling as if calculating, then

nodded her head. Maybe it was better when the fire burned low. Then he couldn't see all the doubt and worry marring her beautiful face.

"Chloe, you're killing me."

She sighed dejectedly. "I went through the packs last night and organized things."

When her pause dragged on, he prompted her. "That's good thinking."

"Well ... you guys sure know how to prepare for an emergency." Her forced smile negated the compliment.

"But?"

She turned her gaze back to the fire, her quiet voice sounding hollow. "I divided the food into three piles. Food I can't eat, food that could make me sick, and food that should be okay."

He scanned the organized gear along the wall. His stomach twisted when his gaze landed on the neatly stacked food. He stomped over and sat in front of them. She'd piled most of the food nicely in one section, food from the MREs he'd eaten more times than he cared to think. The next pile had a few of the plain packages from the MREs with the nutritional sheets set on top. The third pile didn't even have enough for three days. Some food, she must've had in her purse. His pulse pounded in his ears. If they didn't get found, he'd have to watch her starve.

"I'm so sorry, Jake." Her small voice turned his attention to where she still sat, her shoulders slouched and hands twisting in her lap.

He scoffed. "You have nothing to be sorry for."

"I should have been more prepared, carried more

food with me." She gazed back into the fire. "Or better yet, maybe my parents were right. I should just stay where it's safe and not put such stress on everyone I come into contact with."

He hung his head, a pain in his throat he couldn't swallow down. "Chloe, this isn't your fault. I should have taken the storm more seriously, but I've been flying in weather like that my whole life. If we all would have just driven together, this wouldn't have happened."

"You were just trying to keep me safe."

"Lot of good that did." He scrubbed his hand over the back of his neck.

She crawled over to him and grabbed his hand from where it clenched the back of his neck. She threaded her fingers through his and brought their hands under her chin. She smiled a shaky smile that made his stomach turned to stone.

"Listen, there's plenty there. I have enough bars and food I took from the MREs to last at least four days."

He glanced at the small pile of meal replacement bars and foil packages he'd seen a thousand times. The little amount made him sick to his stomach.

"Chloe, that's not enough for a bird." He tried to pull away, but she held on tight.

"Good thing I'm a pixie then." She smiled a genuine smile and kissed his knuckles.

He shook his head and stared at the meager food. His eyes stung, and he blinked to not add more insult to his stupidity. He should've thought the flight through instead of just reacting on emotion.

She leaned up and kissed his cheek. "Stop, Jake. Stop

taking this all on your shoulders. We'll make it. I know you'll get us out of this."

"You don't know that."

"I do. Because you almost killed yourself yesterday getting all this stuff here." She motioned to the supplies lining the walls.

He scoffed. "What a waste of time that turned out to be."

"No, it wasn't." Chloe slid her hand along his shoulders. "We have clothes and sleeping bags to keep us warm, tools and utensils we can use, and food to keep you strong so you can keep us alive. Without all of this, who knows if we'd have made it through the night."

Her confidence in him planted something primal in his heart. He would do whatever needed done—hike all the way back to Steamboat with her on his back if he had to—in order to keep her alive and get out of this mess. He leaned over, wrapped his arm around her back, and pulled her onto his lap. He buried his face into her neck and let her strength and courage seep into him.

"I'm a survivor, Jake Silva," she whispered against his ear as she tightened her arms around him. "And now I have even more to fight for. Mainly, this amazing man who's a survivor, just like me."

She pushed back and peered intently into his eyes. He held perfectly still, not wanting to break whatever spell roped them together. She traced a finger along the scar on his cheek. His hands bunched in the back of her shirt as she followed the trail her finger went with soft kisses. He turned his head and captured her lips with his own, hoping it communicated his promise that they'd persevere.

With a soft moan, she deepened the kiss. Jake's muscles loosened as heat flooded to his fingers and toes. How could he have found a woman who embraced him so completely? He pulled her closer, wanting to hold her tight. He trailed his lips along her jaw and down her neck, sliding his hands up the back of her shirt. She tipped her head back with a sound that both ignited passion, blazing hot in his belly, and snapped his brain to attention.

He needed to stop before this went too far. "Wait ... time out."

He practically dumped her on the floor and scrambled to the other side of the cabin. His breath heaved like he'd just scaled Denali. Pressing his forehead to his hand, he leaned his arm against the log wall, wishing for more than the twelve feet that separated them so he wouldn't have to look at her while he got himself under control.

He glanced over his shoulder. Was she as affected as he was? Her back pressed against the opposite cabin wall like it was the only thing holding her up, and her chest surged with each choppy inhale. Her cheeks had pinked in a deep blush, and her swollen lips tempted him to cross the scant distance between them and dive into her again.

He pushed off the wall and paced like a caged tiger. He didn't want to give up kissing completely, but he needed to lay some ground rules before they continued. Above all else, he had to honor Chloe and God, and if that meant no more kissing, so be it. First, though, he'd try to come up with a compromise.

"New rule." He peeked at her, then slammed his gaze back at the floor in front of him. "Kissing only every three hours."

"What?" Her shocked exclamation puffed his chest up.

Good. He wasn't the only one affected by what was happening between them.

"And only for five minutes." There. That would keep him from crossing the line.

"Seriously?" Chloe pushed off the wall and crossed to him. "We're both adults. I think we can handle more than five minutes."

Her argument held merit. She stepped closer and pressed her petite hand against his pounding heart. He stilled, not trusting himself. She leaned closer, her blue eyes sparkling with mischief. Yep, fairies were definitely trouble.

"No, Chloe, I can't." He stepped back to get some space but came up against the wall. "I keep forgetting myself when I'm with you. I'm not willing to chance dishonoring you or myself."

Her face softened, and her fingers rubbed her neck. "Okay, Jake. We'll play by your rules."

Relief and regret warred within him as his shoulders relaxed.

"So ... our five minutes start now, right?" She stepped closer, her hand trailing up his stomach leaving a line of fire in its wake.

She would be the death of him.

"Have you ever played gin?" His voice strained from his throat.

She tipped her head to the side, her forehead creasing in confusion. "No. I don't think I have."

He grabbed her hand and pulled her to their spot in front of the fire. "Good. I have lots of card games to keep us distracted."

She plopped down on the sleeping bags, muttering something about a better way to stay busy. He rubbed over his heart that pounded furiously in his chest and rushed to his pack for his deck of cards.

Chloe amazed him, and because of her, he no longer wanted to hide behind his scars, pushing people away. When they were found and this stalker issue was over, he wanted to discover the next adventure they'd get through together. The thought buoyed him through the next three hours.

THIRTEEN

The storm rattled the logs of the cabin, causing them to groan as if in pain. Supposedly a person could get used to noises and not notice them anymore, but Chloe didn't think she'd ever get used to the wind as it assaulted the cabin. Would she forever hear the wind howling in her ears, like workers of factories who had the machines they worked with pounding in their heads even after they went home?

She took another small bite of her dinner and chewed the energy bar with deliberate slowness. After scarfing her breakfast down so fast she couldn't remember tasting it, she'd challenged herself to linger over each meal. If she drew it out and chewed until the food disintegrated completely, maybe she'd trick her body into thinking it got more than it actually did. She'd almost failed when the first bite hit her tongue, but she'd held back at the last moment.

Jake scowled at his pasta, pushing it this way and that in the aluminum mug. His anguish at her lack of food had filled the cabin with thick tension all the way to each corner. She'd experienced pity and worry before from other people's reactions to her. She'd never felt such intensity though, not even from Piper, who stayed with her the weeks she was in the hospital and months it took for her to recover.

Chloe didn't think his concern was just a deep-seated sense of duty either. Not with the way he looked at her that settled warm fuzzies in her stomach or the way he stole kisses that burst those warm fuzzies into atomic flames. Something definitely stretched between them she'd never had with anyone else.

Jake's glare at his food deepened, and she laughed. "Just eat it. Please. I'm used to others having food I don't. It's worse for me if you don't eat. Makes me feel guilty."

He huffed and lifted his fork toward his mouth. "Fine." He stopped midway and put the fork back down.

"Jake, seriously, eat."

He shook his head. "What if ..." He stared at her lips before turning back to attacking his meal with his spoon. His neck darkened in the firelight. "Never mind."

Her toes tingled as heat that wasn't from the fire spread up her neck and across her cheeks. The realization hit that he must've heard her conversation with Piper. She narrowed her eyes as she racked her brain for what exactly they had said.

"You know it's rude to listen to other people's conversations."

"I was trained in reconnaissance, Chloe. One of the best there is." He set the cup down.

"What did you hear?"

"Nothing."

"Come on, Jake." She nudged him with her elbow as she turned to face him fully.

"I hadn't meant to. Just, you know, paused outside the door after you called me a beast." He shrugged. "I didn't want to embarrass you."

"Oh, you heard that?" Chloe covered her cheek that had turned from warm to burning hot with the memory of her rant. "I'm sorry. I was just throwing a fit."

"It's okay." His gaze bore into her. "I've been called worse."

He motioned with his finger for her to come closer. Her body responded like he pulled a string wrapped around her. She wasn't sure if she could stop from leaning toward him if she wanted to. Not that she did.

He angled like he would tell her a secret, his lips brushing her ear. "Does my voice still make your toes curl?"

She swallowed, nodding as he kissed along her neck. He straightened with a huff, staring into the fire, and she almost toppled over sideways. She placed her hand on her head and tried to remember what they were discussing.

"I can acquire important intel when I listen in." Jake's sober tone made her breath thick in her chest. "Truthfully, though, I hadn't meant to, but I wouldn't have realized the extent of your celiac if I hadn't. That just touching someone after they've handled gluten could make you sick."

Chloe picked at her shirt hem. "I'm not quite that bad. I'd have to lick my hands or whatever touched them to have a reaction. I'm not about to hide away from the world, though. I just prepare the best I can."

"I'm sorry you have to go through all that." He ran his hand over her cheek.

"I'm not." Her words raised his eyebrows. "I want to use my celiac to help others, Jake, not dwell on it. Eat."

"If we're stuck here, I'm not giving up one of the best parts of being stranded, which is kissing you."

She set her energy bar down, wondering if she could give him a taste of his own medicine. His eyes widened as she turned and moved to her knees. She placed her hands on his cheeks and closed the distance until breath could barely flow between their lips. His hands ran up her back, but he didn't pull her near. She relished that he let her lead without muscling her closer.

"So, you don't want to give up kissing?" Her lips brushed his as she spoke.

The tiny shake of his head made her smile. Now to go in for the kill.

"It's a good thing your packs had toothpaste." She released him and sat back in her spot, though everything in her wanted to follow through with her tease.

He slammed his hand on the floor to keep from falling over. His eyes narrowed and his breath came out choppy.

He scrutinized her. "So, I brush my teeth after eating gluten, and I can still kiss you? You're not just saying this to get me to eat?"

"Brush your teeth, wash your face, and you can kiss me all you want."

Jake's grin looked wolfish as he snatched up his

dinner and ate half of it in one bite. Her toes curled in anticipation, but she kept that to herself. No use stroking his ego more than she already had. She giggled and popped the rest of her measly meal into her mouth.

Jake stood, grabbing their trash and putting it in the plastic bag they'd designated as the garbage. He then began searching through the gear.

"Where did you put that toothpaste again?"

Chloe crossed to the corner pack and pulled out the toothbrushes and toothpaste. His face lit up as he grabbed one and went to brushing his teeth. He scrubbed and scrubbed until Chloe worried he wouldn't have any enamel left. After spitting into the fire, he opened the door, scooped a mug of snow from the already accumulating pile, and rubbed the snow vigorously across his lips, then over his entire face. He then strode to his backpack, pulled out hand sanitizer, and smeared it across his lips.

She tipped her head back and laughed. "That's more than sufficient."

How could her heart feel so light when their situation remained dire? He took two gigantic steps and swooped her up in his arms. His deep kiss tasted of toothpaste and sanitizer and made her heart beat like a track full of racing horses. He pulled her closer, lifting her off the floor so her feet dangled. She shrieked and smiled big against his lips. This man was amazing.

He set her down and leaned back, rubbing one hand across his lips. "They're stinging."

Chloe snorted and stepped away. "Hand sanitizer on the face might not be the best thing."

"I'm not sure if it's that or your kisses, but it was worth it," Jake whispered before heading to the woodpile to add more wood to the fire.

She moved back to their nest of sleeping bags and sat down. After throwing one more log onto the fire, Jake limped back to her. He still hadn't taken off his prosthetic, and she worried about his reason. She bit the inside of her mouth, warring with herself. Should she ask him or leave it be?

He sat close to her and lifted her hand into his, closing his fingers around hers. He leaned against the packs they used as backrests, lazily drawing swirls on the back of her hand with his free hand. They'd kept themselves busy with reorganizing the packs and playing cards with a deck he had in his backpack, but just sitting here, staring into the fire might be her favorite part of the day yet. Aside from kissing and waking up in his strong arms.

She peeked at his profile and forced her anxiety down. "Jake?"

"Huh?"

"Why don't you take off your prosthetic and get comfortable?" She tried to keep her tone light when his fingers flinched in hers. "It's not like we're going anywhere, anytime soon."

"We might need to leave quickly." He cleared his throat and shifted. "It's better if I keep it on."

Was he going to trust her enough to let her in? What did it mean if he didn't? He'd shown throughout this entire ordeal that he cared for her on some level. She wanted to show him she cared for him too, not despite his injury, but because of it. He'd overcome so much that it gave her hope she could become just as strong. She wanted more than false bravado.

She had to start somewhere. She mentally pulled on her big girl panties and sat on his lap so she could look straight into his face. He crossed his arms, his mouth drawn into a straight line.

"You are the most amazing man I've ever known, Jake Silva. When I'm with you, I want to be brave and strong, to not just bury my fears but kick them into the stratosphere."

His arms loosened a little, and the harsh line of his lips relaxed.

"If you don't think there's something more for us beyond this time we're stuck here, then I guess you can hide from me."

At that, he dropped his hands to her waist and shook his head. "Chloe—"

She pressed her hands to his chest. "But I don't want to hide anything from you, Jake. I'm not afraid you'll see my ugly parts of life and turn away, because you've been there."

That last bit wasn't completely truthful, but she wouldn't take it back. She doubted she'd ever truly have the confidence to let that fear go completely. The inevitable moment when her health would wedge between her relationships. She shook off the heaviness and plunged forward.

"Please, trust me like I trust you. Let me see you, Jake. The real you."

His brows lowered as he stared at her. He was quiet for so long she thought she'd made him mad. When he nodded, one curt nod, her mouth went dry, and she blinked the moisture from behind her eyelids.

He moved his legs, and she hurried off to kneel beside his left side, though she wanted to show her relief and gratitude with a kiss. He winced as he pulled up his pants and bent his leg. She hadn't expected the intricate design of the limb.

"Wow, that's fancy." She darted a look his way to make sure she hadn't offended him.

He swallowed and cleared his throat. "Yeah. My friend's wife, June, has spent a lot of time improving prosthetic limbs to make them better."

He unbuckled the strap around his thigh and pulled off the leg with a sigh. He gazed at it a moment before handing it to her. She turned it this way and that, trying not to stare as he slipped the protective sock from his skin. The prosthetic really was incredible, and she could see how the design could help in his range of movement.

She lowered the leg to ask him a question, but it stalled in her brain at the sight of his angry, red skin. "Oh, Jake."

She set the foot aside and reached for his leg. He flinched and jerked it away.

"How bad does it hurt?" she whispered.

"It's just the muscle, like when you work out too much at the gym."

She doubted that but wasn't about to push him. An idea popped into her head. She rushed over to her purse and started digging around in it.

"I have something I think will help." She pulled out the tube of ointment and hurried back over. Kneeling at his feet so he couldn't snatch it from her, she held the tube up. "I can't take conventional pain killers, which is a bummer for someone as clumsy as I am. But this arnica ointment seems to help."

She squeezed some in her hand and reached for his leg.

"Chloe—"

She glared at him to get him to relax, then trailed her fingers along the smooth skin. She wasn't sure what she had expected, but there wasn't a lot of scarring that she could see in the firelight, just a rounded end where the calf should be. Why was he so hesitant to show her this?

She rubbed her hands together to warm up the ointment and smiled at him. "Don't want to hear you yelp from the freezing stuff."

He didn't smile, just bore a hole through her with his intense stare. He'd pressed his knuckles to the floor like he would bolt in a split second. His entire upper body radiated tension.

"Tell me if I hurt you." She put her hands on his knee and worked her way down his leg.

When the ointment ran out, she squeezed some more into her hand, warmed it up, and continued to massage it in. Little by little, his arms relaxed.

"How were you injured?" She slowed her motions, rubbing languid, circular motions and peering into his face.

He swallowed and cleared his throat. "We were in South America rescuing a family that had been kidnapped. We found them being held hostage in an old hay storage off the side of a barn. When we engaged, the entire area erupted into chaos."

Jake stared into the fire, his tone even as he retold the story. Chloe focused on keeping her motions smooth and slow, afraid any sudden movement would zip his lips back up tight.

"We were too late to save the husband and wife. We snatched up their little girl and hightailed it back to the chopper." Jake rubbed his hands through his hair. "We were about a half a klick out when I saw movement in the trees. It was like the dude just materialized out of nowhere. I hate the jungle."

"So, no tropical vacations for us, huh?" She smiled what she hoped was encouraging. "Maybe we could just stay on the beach, lounge around in our swimsuits, and swim in the ocean then?"

"I think I could do that."

"Good. I could go for a nice, warm vacation when this is all over with." She sobered. "What happened next?"

"My friend Sosimo didn't see the combatant, so I jumped between him and the enemy and tackled Sosimo to the ground. Went to get up and couldn't. I'd been shot twice. Once in the calf, shattering the bone. Another in the thigh. It hit the artery there. I almost bled out before we got halfway to base. Of course, I don't remember anything past bouncing against Sosimo's back, fending off attackers as they popped out of the forest like ants out of an anthill."

Sharp pain speared through Chloe's chest as the

images raced through her head. The pain he must've been in and how he had still protected his friend.

"They were using armor-piercing rounds. Killed Ethan Stryker. Sometimes I wish they would've killed me too."

"No." Chloe shook her head, crawled up onto his lap, and placed her hands on his cheek. "I know how that feels, lying in the hospital, wondering what's the point of fighting. Then you get home, only to find your dreams have evaporated to leave pain behind and a life full of constant struggles. I know that despair, and I refuse to live in that. And I'm not letting you camp there either."

"You say you want to be brave? I think you've got more bravery than anyone I know. So much more than I have." Jake knocked his head on the pack behind him.

She leaned forward, her lips brushing against his. "That's why we are so perfect together." She pressed her mouth to his softly, ignoring the fact that it wasn't Kissing Time. "I can help you realize how amazing you are." She nibbled on his lower lip. "And you make me feel like maybe not all of my dreams were lost in the wind."

Jake groaned and captured her lips, devouring her like he'd been starving for days. She felt like she'd barely lived before him, surviving on scraps of what life could really be. His arms banded around her and pulled her even closer. Her chest swelled and bloomed with love like a field of a million wildflowers bursting into color all at once.

FOURTEEN

Snow blew all around Jake as he pushed against the wind that battered him. He scanned left and right, searching. His heart pounded in his throat. Failure whispered in his ear.

"Chloe!" The storm whipped his yell up to the clouds.

A gust blew white so thick he couldn't see his hand in front of his face. The wind knocked him in the back, throwing him into the frigid snow. He scrambled to his feet, knowing if he failed, she'd die.

A dark shape formed ahead of him, and his feet slipped in his haste to get to her. He pulled up short when the wind died and the snow stopped to reveal a man in a black coat with the hood pulled up. His hand tightened around Chloe's neck as he held her against him.

Chloe struggled and whimpered, pleading with her eyes for Jake to save her.

Jake took a step forward, his heart threatening to pound out of his chest. The man lifted a gun at Jake's head. Jake narrowed his eyes, daring the man.

A deep chuckle raced shivers down Jake's spine as the man moved the gun to Chloe's head. "Didn't I say you'd regret it?"

"Chloe!"

Jake stepped forward, but his prosthetic slipped off, crashing him into the snowbank. He roared as the wind picked back up, blinding him from Chloe. Her terrified scream filled the air, swirling around him in surround sound, slicing into his chest and ripping his heart out.

"No!" he woke up bellowing, his arms flailing and throwing Chloe off of him as he sat up with a jerk.

He tried to orient himself, but the dream raged in his head.

"Jake." Chloe cringed as she crawled to him, her eyes wide on her petite face.

He held up his hands, warding her off, but she pushed them aside and placed her small hand on his cheek. Her face was pale in the soft firelight, and her hand shook against his cheek. Her fear gutted him. He gulped, sucking in air like all the oxygen had disappeared.

"He had you." He couldn't breathe. Couldn't focus.

"It's okay. It was just a dream."

Jake shook his head and closed his eyes. He'd failed her. Hadn't been enough. His throat closed with a sharp pain.

"Jake, look at me."

He squeezed his eyes tighter. He couldn't see the pity and disappointment in her eyes. She grabbed his hand.

"Jake Silva, you look at me right now."

She squeezed his hand with more strength than he thought possible, and he forced his eyes open. She took his hand, kissed the palm, and placed it against her cheek. Then she reached for his other hand and pressed it against her heart.

"I'm okay. It was just a dream."

"I couldn't get to you," he stammered. "I failed. Wasn't enough."

"You will always be enough." She leaned forward and gave him a tender kiss that broke the terror loose.

She was here and fine, for the most part. He pulled her back to him when she moved away, sliding his hand along her cheek and threading his fingers into her short hair. She wrapped her arms around him and sighed. The sound blasted the ice that had encased his heart and spread flames through his body. He brought his other hand up to her hair, needing the softness against his rough fingers.

She winced and sucked in a hissing breath. What in the world? He pulled his hand away, his fingers sticky with blood.

"What?" He pulled her around and eased the hair aside to reveal a gash with a bump already forming.

"It's nothing." Chloe pushed his hand away and tried to face him.

"That's not nothing." He turned her back around and examined the wound more closely. "What happened?"

She huffed. Her exasperation would have been funny if the situation wasn't so serious. "I think I knocked my head on one of the stones."

His fingers stilled and turned to ice. "I hurt you?" He yanked his hands away, already knowing the answer.

"No."

"Yes, yes I did." His voice came out harsh and louder than he expected, making her flinch. "I knew this would happen."

"You didn't mean to." She reached for him.

He scrambled up, hopping twice to steady himself on the cabin wall. She bit her bottom lip and got to her knees. Hurt filled her dark blue eyes.

"Don't you get it? I'd never mean to hurt you." Jake leaned against the wall and gestured toward the fireplace. "I'll just throw you across the room, knock you senseless, and almost catch you on fire."

Chloe shot to her feet. "You're being a little dramatic, don't you think?" She crossed her arms over her chest that rose and fell.

"Chloe, you're bleeding. Nothing dramatic about that."

"Well, next time you start jabbering in your sleep, I'll know to wake you up."

"Yeah, and instead of me tossing you around, I'll end up choking you out, thinking you're attacking me." He smiled unkindly as the color drained from her face. "Not so dramatic now, huh?"

Her lips flattened and eyes narrowed. Man, she was beautiful when she was angry. He steeled his heart against her.

"Doesn't matter, anyway." He tore his gaze from her and leaned his head against the rough log wall. "We'll be sleeping on opposite sides of the cabin from here on out."

He couldn't risk having her close. Couldn't let sleep pull him under without her being safe from him. He'd just keep his distance, and he couldn't hurt her again.

"Aagh." Her growl popped his eyes open to where she stood.

She stomped up to him, arms flailing, and poked him in the chest. Hard. He barely contained the urge to rub it.

"So, what? You're done with me now?" The anger didn't cover the hurt in her voice.

No. Yes. He swallowed. "I can't risk hurting you."

"You may be scared, Silva." She poked him again. "But I'm not. This is those ugly parts I was talking about, or were you not listening?"

He gave in and rubbed his chest. "I was listening."

"So, then you're just dense?" She cocked her blonde eyebrow at him.

He glared. "No, just realistic."

"Well, how about this for reality? I know you're afraid, that you don't want me to see you like this. And I get that." She paused and swallowed, the anger on her face softening. "Do you think I want you to see me writhing in pain, stuck on the floor in front of the toilet? Do you think I'm afraid of you tiring of taking care of me, of your plans being ruined yet again because I'm too sick to do anything?"

He shook his head. He'd never hold that against her. "You can't help that."

"And you can help yours?"

"Your problems won't leave me bruised and bloody." He roared in her face, hoping—praying—he'd scare her enough to back away and forget him.

She stepped closer, placing a hand on his chest. "No, mine will just tear at your heart one piece at a time until you're left with nothing but vague memories of a full life." She laughed humorlessly. "Maybe we are better alone."

He clenched his hands at his side. The idea of life without her stabbed him in the heart. The thought of her alone ripped it in two.

She circled the other hand around his waist. "I don't want to be alone anymore, Jake. But I have a dilemma, because I don't want to be with anyone but you."

He placed his hands on her hips, knowing he should push her away. "You deserve someone better than me."

"You really haven't been listening, have you? It's you or no one. No one else will ever come close to comparing to you."

He groaned, his fingers flexing. "Chloe, I need so much help."

"I need help, too. I've been too scared to get it." She leaned against him, pushing him into the logs. "But if you're with me, I don't think I'll be so scared."

He spread his hands across her back, leaning his forehead against hers. "I ... I think it'd help to have you with me too."

He pulled her close, amazed at her unwillingness to give up. How many times had he pushed his desires aside since that mission, believing no woman would want to deal with his issues and lacks? Yet, here she stood, forcing him to see his strengths, knowing that they could build on those to overcome both of their weaknesses. Though doubts still whispered deep in his soul, he wanted to focus on the hope Chloe voiced.

FIFTEEN

Three days after the crash, Chloe laid her head on Jake's lap, examining the cards in her hand. Well, really, she stared at Jake over the top of her hand, her cards blurring to red and black. She loved how his eyebrows would furrow as he shifted cards around. How his mouth would tick up just the slightest bit on the right side when he had a great hand. When he had a dud set of cards, he'd chew the inside of his cheek. Most people probably wouldn't even notice the minuscule movement, but she'd caught on to it sometime the day before.

Her hands shook, so she set her cards on her chest, hoping she masked the evidence of her hunger quickly enough. Why hide behind cards, anyway, when one could stare openly? Besides, she'd tired of cards hours ago. He'd taught her so many new games, the rules jumbled in her head.

When she asked where he'd learned them all, he'd talked about all the spare time he had in the Army waiting for a mission to come. Hours and days of boredom interrupted by moments of pure adrenaline rush. It probably meant this idleness didn't drive him batty, unlike her. If she didn't have a gorgeous man to stare at, she probably would run into the blizzard, just for some excitement. She bit her lip. Maybe she could convince Jake to put the game aside for some more kissing.

Jake's lips flattened as his neck turned red. "Chloe, if you keep staring at me like that, I'll never be able to beat you at this game."

"That's okay." Chloe walked her fingers up his shirt. "I'm ready for a more diverting form of entertainment anyway."

Jake groaned and tossed his cards into the discard pile. "We still have an hour and thirty-six minutes."

Chloe huffed and set her cards in the pile with his. "That really was a lame-brain rule to make, you know."

While she'd hated Jake's stupid rule, she saw the virtue in it and loved him even more for insisting on keeping what she had named Kissing Time. Though, when he upped the make-out time to ten minutes, she'd done a happy dance around the cabin.

Now here she lay, with an hour and thirty-six minutes to wait. He stared long and deep into her eyes, his finger tracing her bottom lip before sliding along her cheek. Every place his finger trailed tingled like his fingers radiated electricity. She closed her eyes to savor the sensation.

"Necessary rule. Very, very necessary." Jake's deep, gritty voice made her smile knowingly as she opened her eyes.

She turned her face into his hand and kissed his palm, then rolled over so she faced the fire. Their mountain of wood had dwindled to a small stack, and the low embers they kept the fire at didn't produce a lot of light. While she loved this time getting to know Jake, the hours dragged on and the disappointment of missing the concert had her struggling to keep positive. How much longer could she stay out here, handsome man or not, without letting the melancholy drag her under?

"I could stay here forever." Jake's statement seemed to echo in the small cabin.

She couldn't tell if his words or the way his fingers combed through her hair caused the shiver that ran through her. "Why is that?"

"One, I have you all to myself." His finger traced her ear, and she decided his touch caused the shiver. "Two, since the mission ... I just kind of hate being around people."

Her mouth went dry, and she tried to remain relaxed. She'd always been a people person, loving meeting new friends. Since her time in the hospital, she fed off of others' energy even more, sometimes just going to a coffee shop so she could experience people's emotions as she sat and watched. It was the main reason she loved performing so much. All that joy and excitement of the crowd would rush through her like a shot of liquid energy that kept her going for weeks. The thought of him hating being around people troubled her.

"Why is that?" She hoped her voice didn't convey her worry.

Chloe felt his shrug in his arms and rolled onto her

back to see his face. His Adam's apple bobbed with his hard swallow and his fingers trembled softly as he ran them through her hair. He didn't look down at her, just stared into the fire, and Chloe's heart clenched.

"I guess ... I got tired of the scared looks I always get." He cleared his throat. "Figured it was better to stay away from others than to have them afraid of me."

Chloe couldn't imagine anyone ever being afraid of him. Well, maybe if he scowled he might make people nervous. She lifted her hand to his scarred cheek and pushed her fingers along his scar.

"Could you have misunderstood their reactions?" she asked softly, not wanting to add more hurt on him.

"Always the optimist?" He grinned sadly down at her, and she shrugged. "You didn't see their faces. Didn't watch them flinch away."

"You didn't scare me."

"You're unique. Extraordinary." He placed his hand on hers, pressing them harder against his cheek.

His compliment filled her with warmth and made her lightheaded. It also made her think about when she'd first opened the door back in Steamboat. He'd appeared so serious, so intense.

"Did you smile?" The words blurted out.

He scoffed and rolled his eyes. "What does that have to do with anything?"

She shrugged. "They may have been more scared of your scowl than anything else. It's a little intimidating."

He curled his fingers around hers and stared down at her. He fiddled with her rings while he thought. He licked his lips and gazed back into the fire.

"No, I don't think so," he muttered low, and her heart sank.

"So ... you don't go places?"

"Only for jobs, otherwise I just stick to the ranch. Can't scare people if I don't go anywhere."

Chloe's mind floundered. What would that mean for them when they got out of this situation? How could he stay stuck at home all the time? She'd wither away if she had to stay cooped up at a ranch, no matter how beautiful. Granted, if she was with Jake, she didn't need the rush of people as much. He energized her more than a million lightning bolts. But she still wanted to sing, to fill a crowd with joy and anticipation. She could find a way to have both Jake the Recluse and the thrill of the stage, maybe even show him he pictured himself all wrong.

"Didn't you say your friend got married recently?" She prayed for the right words as he nodded, wondering if she could get him to not be so hard on himself. "Doesn't she have a kid?"

He's eyes narrowed, and his voice sounded hesitant. "Yeah, so?"

"How did they react to you?"

His forehead pinched together as he stared into space. Chloe bit the inside of her cheeks so she'd keep her mouth shut and let him think. Tears welled behind her eyelids as his forehead smoothed and a slight smile lifted the corners of his mouth. He squeezed her hand and rubbed her knuckles across his lips.

"What?" The need to share in his revelation was intense within her chest.

"Eva, Samantha's daughter, asked if I was a prince." He scoffed and rolled his eyes.

Chloe's wide smile hurt her cheeks. "She did? Why'd she think that?"

Jake's neck and ears turned red, causing her eyebrows to rise in amazement. "She claimed I was the prettiest of all, so I had to be a prince."

Chloe giggled, covering her mouth with her free hand.

"I guess she and I will get hitched when she grows up." Jake's deep chuckle had Chloe's toes curling. "She probably doesn't realize I'll be pushing ancient by that time."

Chloe sat up and sat on Jake's lap so she could see his expression in the darkened room, and placed her hands on his shoulders to steady herself. "So, I have some steep competition I need to worry about?"

"No. No competition at all." Jake's fingers dug into her hips.

"Did she say this after she'd known you for a while?" Chloe toyed with his hair, her lips tipping at the fact that he had longer hair than she did.

"No. We had just met. I was sitting out on the porch at the ranch, and she climbed right up into my lap without asking and pushed her book into my hand." Jake's eyes radiated joy and lingering surprise. "Man, I miss her."

"So if this darling child wasn't afraid of you, is there a possibility that you've been seeing things wrong?"

His shoulders slumped with his sigh. "Chloe, you haven't seen what I have."

"You're right. I wasn't scared of you. No one at the places we went in Steamboat seemed afraid of you, either. If anything, the women seemed interested." She huffed and pushed out her lower lip. "I didn't like that part. Not at all."

"You didn't like me at that point."

"I liked you from the moment I opened the door."

"Whatever."

Chloe looked at a spot on his neck, nervous about her next question. "So, would you want to be around people if you didn't scare them?"

"Why are you pushing this?" His gruff voice caused her stomach to flutter.

She shrugged and moved to go throw another log on the fire. "No reason."

"Chloe." He gripped her hips, keeping her from running away.

She pulled at his hoodie string, not wanting to say what worried her, but knowing it wasn't fair to hold back. "I guess I'm just wondering what will happen when I have to go for shows."

"I don't understand." He lifted her chin.

"I'm gone a lot, traveling for concerts. In fact, I don't even live in Colorado." She licked her lips. "You don't like leaving your ranch."

He cupped his hand behind her neck. "We don't have to figure all that out right now."

She nodded, swallowing the pain in her throat. He leaned forward and brushed his lips against hers.

"Let's not worry about the details, okay?" He kissed her again, and she determined to push the doubt aside.

"What about the make-out rule? We still have over an hour until Kissing Time." She pulled away, but not far enough to discourage him.

"I call a time-out on that stupid rule." He growled and pulled her back to him.

She laughed against his mouth, though doubt still pulled at her heart. Obviously, he wouldn't be declaring his undying love anytime soon. He probably was right, though. She would process all this much better when she had a full stomach. For now, she'd focus on surviving. Once they got rescued, she'd focus on the rest. She fisted her hands in his sweatshirt, determined to make the next ten minutes of kissing earth shaking.

SIXTEEN

"Do you hear that?" Chloe startled Jake from his after-noon nap.

He usually wasn't one for napping away the after-noon, but after three days of food rationing, he figured storing his energy was an important endeavor. Plus, then he got to hold Chloe close since she wouldn't listen to reason and stay away from him.

"What?" He sat up, cocking his head. Was it a plane? Helicopter, maybe?

"Nothing. I don't hear anything." Chloe smiled at him from eyes bruised black with lack of food. "Has the storm passed?"

Jake slipped on his prosthetic, still amazed that his ugly stump hadn't affected her at all, and rushed to the door. The snow sparkled in the bright sunlight, lifting his spirits that soon they'd be rescued. He still wouldn't bank on it, though. He knew how hard triangulating a location could be, especially in mountains like these.

Chloe tucked herself against him, wrapping her arms around his waist. "It's so beautiful."

He surveyed the clear slope and the treeless valley past the trees that protected the cabin. The storm had covered the plane in snow, but he could still make out the wing where it tipped into the sky. It really had been a miracle they'd found this smooth place to land when all the surrounding area was covered in the thick wilderness forest.

He kissed the top of Chloe's head and turned to the cabin. "Yep. I'm going to go set the traps in the forest, grab some more wood, then see if I can get in the airplane and unload the rest of the packs in there."

"What can I do to help?" Chloe moved to her winter gear, bending to pull on her boots.

His stomach knotted, and he hoped she'd take his request without fussing. "You can help by conserving your energy and keeping the fire going."

She paused, her foot halfway in the boot. "But I want to get out of here. I'm fine, Jake, really."

"I know, honey. I know." He ran his hand through his hair. "But we can't have you wasting energy you can't afford to blow through. We aren't sure how long we'll be out here."

Her shoulders slumped, her head bowing to her knees. She wasn't like him, content to sit and stare at the fire, playing cards. The Army had trained him well for boredom. He could fix this, though.

He lowered himself next to her. "Listen, let me go take care of these essentials, then when I'm done, we'll bundle up and snuggle on the front porch. We can watch the sunset over the mountains."

She turned her head and rested her cheek on her knee. "Only if you agree to kiss me while we're snuggling."

His heart picked up its beat, pounding wildly in his chest. Man, he loved how she affected him.

"Deal." He pushed the word past the emotion in his throat.

She leaned forward and kissed his lips before pulling back and waving him away. "Go slay dragons and other manly things."

He smiled. "I'll be back." He kissed her one more time with a kiss that seared his insides.

He pulled away, reluctance to leave her heavy in his stomach. How would he be able to have her gone for months at a time? Could he leave his family at Stryker Security? He looked back as he pulled the door closed. She'd bundled back up into the sleeping bag and lain before the fire. Her hair stuck out on her head, probably from his obsession with running his fingers through it. While her bright blue eyes looked tired, they still sparkled at him from her face. Yeah, he'd follow her to the other side of the world if she let him.

"Go, Jake."

Her laughter tempted him to stomp back in and curl up with her, but this break in the weather may be just a temporary reprieve. He closed the door, slipped on his snowshoes, and headed into the forest. The storm had dumped a lot of snow, blowing drifts against the brush and boulders. He only walked fifty yards before he saw what he searched for.

The prints of rabbits emerging from their burrows crisscrossed the snow like a chaotic map. He located four busier paths and set up the snares he'd fashioned out of paracord. Hopefully, when he came back to check it just before nightfall, there'd be fat rabbits he could feed Chloe with. He took a deep breath, inhaling the clean scent of a forest after fresh snow, and steeled himself for the next task.

He trekked closer to the cabin to get wood. The birds twittered their joyful song in the branches above him. Leaning his hand against a tree, he gulped his breaths, his energy waning more than he wanted to admit. He needed to get to the plane, even if it was just to dig all the food out of the packs left in there. Anything he trapped in his snares would go to Chloe, so he'd need the energy the MREs left in the plane would provide to keep her alive.

First, though, he had to focus on wood. They could live more days without food than they could heat and melted snow. He took the hatchet she'd found and whacked it against the base of the tree. Three more whacks, and the tree fell with a thump. He pulled it up to the side of the cabin and turned to get another. The *thunk, thunk* of the metal echoed through the valley as he felled two more trees.

He squared the head of the hatchet on the last tree he'd take today and hit it with as much strength as he could. He'd have to take a brief break when he finished with this to recoup some energy. Maybe check on Chloe.

The echo from the hit quieted, but a distant crack had Jake scanning the sky through the thick treetops. A low rumbling like a thunderstorm built behind the mountain ridge, though the sky was blue as far as he could see. He headed toward the cabin to get a clearer look, when the sound intensified like a jet taking off an aircraft carrier.

Jake's stomach flipped. Avalanche. The treeless valley suddenly made sense. He took off for the cabin. The snowshoe on the prosthetic caught in the trees he'd just cut down, twisting off his leg and throwing him headfirst into the cold.

Snow billowed around him, filling his nose and mouth. Somehow he recognized he wasn't in the thick of the avalanche, but the thought of being buried alive had him moving. He scrambled on his hands and knees to the side of the cabin. Pushing himself up against the log walls, he stood, praying the onslaught of thick snow would stop.

Chloe's screams threaded through the thundering mountain and sliced into his heart. His chest heaved as the rumbling slowed and the birds' chirping renewed. Only a heavy cloud of settling snow remained from the violent last minute raged by the avalanche.

Jake hopped to the corner of the cabin and slumped. The plane, which held supplies they'd need to make it and the emergency beacon, no longer sat where he'd crashed it. The mountain had swept it away and buried it deep within an expanse of hard-packed snow.

He needed to get the wood chopped now so he could search for the wreckage. He went to his knees and crawled to where his foot had gotten stuck. He pulled it from the log it had wedged beneath, and with a sick feeling in his stomach, the foot flopped awkwardly from the ankle. His muscles quivered as his gut hardened. Because of him and his inabilities, Chloe would die. A guttural roar ripped from his chest and bounced through the valley.

———————

"JAKE, IT'S NOT YOUR FAULT," Chloe stated for the hundredth time as she grabbed wood from the pile he'd thrown near the cabin.

When the avalanche had reverberated through the cabin, she thought for sure she'd end up buried alive in the shack from hell. She'd also known she didn't care, since Jake had to have been swept away in the raging snow.

As the thundering had slowed to quiet, she had curled into a ball before the fire, great sobs wracking her body. Jake's primal scream had sent shivers down her spine and rushed her body with relief so fast she thought she'd faint. She'd found him white from head to toe, his broken prosthetic tossed aside. At that moment, she knew she'd give up whatever she had to, even her career, if it meant staying with him.

Jake's disgruntled humph before he turned back to chopping the last tree raised all her hackles. She'd tried to get him to come inside and rest, but he'd pushed her off, muscled one of the fallen trees beside a rock, and while resting the knee of his injured leg on the rock, began chopping the tree into firewood. She'd forced him to drink some water and had refused to go back inside when he growled at her.

She had a stubborn tenacity to rival a mule. Something Jake would get well acquainted with, especially if he kept acting like an idiot. An anguished idiot who took far too much on his own shoulders and impressed her with every awkward, balanced chop of the ax. She just wanted to take a minute to hug him, to reassure him that everything would work out.

Yet Chloe didn't know that for sure, so she held back. Maybe he just needed time to get his frustration out. She looked through the trees at the expanse of white where the airplane had landed. She snorted. She sure picked the perfect place to land. Avalanche Alley. All the snow that had fallen during the storm must have layered just right on the ridge. Thankfully, whoever built the cabin had tucked it inside the trees, otherwise the entire thing would've been swept away like the plane. She shuddered at the thought and rushed to take the stack of wood in her arms inside.

Two more loads and Jake followed her inside and slumped to the floor in a dejected pile of grumbling male ego. The cabin once again had a mountain of wood to keep the fire going. Technically, if they were wise about the wood use, they could survive at least another fourteen days. Wasn't that how long a person could live without food? She prayed it didn't come to that.

She took a mug of water to Jake and pushed it into his hand. He gave a half-hearted grunt that had Chloe's eyes rolling. This forced vacation would get old fast if he didn't snap out of it.

Stomping to the other side of the cabin, she wished the room had just a few more square-feet to show her upset. Two steps just didn't seem to hold the punch she wanted. She may have to resort to actually throwing a fist. Maybe then he'd wake up.

She grabbed their dinner, knowing the day hadn't gotten to that time yet, but also knowing Jake had used a lot of energy stripping the forest of its trees. She stomped back to him for good measure and flopped down beside him. She shoved his cold pack of gelatinous spaghetti at him. That meal hadn't tempted her like the rest.

"I don't want it." Jake's low grumble irked her.

"Don't be an idiot."

"Too late for that."

"You just used every calorie you've consumed since we got here. Eat." She poked him in the side.

He hmphed and squeezed a bite into his mouth. Chloe took a bite of her bar, the sweetness soothing her frazzled nerves. She took another bite and closed her eyes while she chewed. The wood crackled in the fireplace. Birds chirped happily outside. The stink of sweat and self-loathing waved off of Jake.

"You have to stop. This funk isn't going to help us any." Chloe peeked over at him as she took another bite.

"I should've known. It's so obvious this is an avalanche chute."

"Jake, please. We were crashing. It's not like you could be picky." Chloe balled her wrapper up and put it in the garbage bag. "Besides, this cabin has been a Godsend. It would've been hard to survive that storm without it."

He shrugged and took another bite. Men. She drank the mug of water down in four big gulps and went outside to get some more snow. When she got back in, she set the mug by the fire to melt and lay down on the sleeping bag. Hauling the wood had zapped her energy to nil.

She touched his leg, and he flinched. "Can you lay with me for a little bit? I need to rest before we tackle the next task."

His gaze darted to her and back to the fire. With a slight shake of the head, his refusal squeezed her heart. She narrowed her eyes. He wasn't getting off that easy.

"Please, I'm cold." Ugh, that tone was annoying.

"I'll get you another sleeping bag."

She bit her tongue to keep from calling him an idiot again. That probably wouldn't turn his attitude around. Could she appeal to his inner hero when he had entrenched himself in such a deep pit of anger?

"I don't want a sleeping bag."

"Chloe, I—"

"The truth is, I'm still scared ... still shaking from thinking you'd been buried alive."

She closed her eyes to that thought, her nose stinging. Shoot. She hadn't meant to get all weepy, but the afternoon crashed over her. She couldn't stop from tearing up. She cleared her throat, yet the emotion wouldn't dislodge.

"I just ... I just need you to hold me, or do you not want to do that anymore?"

He stared down at her, his eyebrows pushing together and his eyes shining with doubt. He opened his mouth only to snap it shut with a small shake of his head. Why was he so hesitant to be with her? Had the snow swept away his growing affection like it had the plane?

With a deep sigh, he lay down beside her. She scooted close, wrapping her arms tightly around him and burying her face in his neck. It was pathetic and weak, but she didn't care. She needed his arms holding her. Needed the assurance that they'd survived another harrowing day.

SEVENTEEN

Anguished mutterings pulled Chloe out of sleep. She blinked groggily as she tried to focus on the noise. Jake's arms tightened around her. His fingers dug into her muscles and woke her fully.

"No." The pain in his voice twisted her heart.

How could she wake him without startling him like before? She levered herself onto her elbows and studied his face in the dim light. His heart beat hard against her hand and sweat beaded on his forehead.

She leaned down and brushed her lips like butterfly wings against his. She crooned "It Is Well With My Soul," the first hymn that popped into her head.

"Jake." She kept her voice low and kissed him again. "Jake, wake up."

His forehead relaxed, and he turned toward her. The corners of her mouth twitched as warmth spread up her cheeks. She touched her lips to his with more pressure.

"Wake up, Jake. It's kissing time."

Strong fingers eased and stretched across her back. His body relaxed. She smiled against his lips and pressed them more firmly to his. That she could tame the beast that haunted him in his sleep had her flying as high as the mountaintop. She scooted up further to get a better angle.

His groan as he slid his hands up her back and dug his fingers into her hair had blood rushing to her ears in a deafening beat. Relief that he responded to her made her giggle against his lips. The uncertainty of earlier gave way to a happiness she hadn't felt before.

He froze, his eyes popping open and his eyebrows flying to his hairline. "Ch—Chloe?"

"You expecting someone else?" She smirked and leaned down to continue their make-out session.

He put his fingers over her lips, stopping her descent. "I didn't brush my teeth." Sitting fast, he muttered low, "So stupid."

He reached for the cup of water and a scrap of fabric and scrubbed at her lips hard. She winced and pulled at his hands. He glared and shoved the cup into her hands while he crawled to the Ziplock bag with their tooth-brushes.

"Jake, its o—"

"It's not okay." He squeezed toothpaste onto the bristles. "I can't even kiss you without screwing up."

Chloe rolled her eyes as she snatched the toothbrush from his hand. "I believe I was the one kissing you."

She brushed her teeth with vigorous strokes, taking her frustration out on her enamel. Why the man insisted on infuriating her was beyond understanding. She spit into the fire and pointed to his toothbrush with a lift of one eyebrow.

He shook his head and turned to put them away.

Anger and hurt heated her cheeks. She tossed her toothbrush at him, pegging him in the shoulder. He glanced down at where the brush had landed and up at her with a questioning look on his face.

"Get over it, Jake." She crossed her arms over her chest.

"Get over what exactly? Being reckless with your safety and flying us into a storm we had no business going into? How about that every decision I make makes matters worse for you?" Jake speared his hand into his hair. "I can't even kiss you without screwing up."

"I know I'm a hassle."

"That's an understatement."

His words hit her like a slap across the face. She flinched and curled in on herself, turning toward the fire. Hadn't she already known she was too much trouble? She never should've gotten her hopes up. Should've kept the guard around her heart that allowed it to remain intact.

"Chloe, I didn't ... that's not what I meant." He shifted behind her.

"Yes, it is." Chloe glanced at her watch. "It shouldn't be dark yet." She moved to the snow pants and pushed her legs through them in jerky motions. "I'm going to go check the snares."

"Chloe, wait."

She shoved her feet into her boots and rushed out of the cabin, grabbing her coat and the snowshoes on the way out. She wiped the tears that streamed down her face with a growl and took off into the woods. Coward.

The light faded from the sky. While colors hadn't painted the landscape in the pinks, purples, and oranges of sunset yet, she couldn't imagine it was far off. She followed the indentions of Jake's footprints from earlier. While the avalanche had swept away everything in the valley, it had just dusted below the trees slightly with its cloud of snow. Thankfully, she could still make out Jake's footsteps in the waning light.

"Fool." What was she thinking, believing someone as amazing as Jake would want to deal with her?

It was probably better that it came out now than after they got rescued. She stopped, bending over at the sharp pain in her heart. Shaking it off, she continued trekking through the woods, muttering to herself.

She pulled up short at the sight of a rabbit lying beneath the brush. She covered her mouth and did a little happy dance. The thought of roasted rabbit had her mouth watering. She rushed to pull the animal out of the trap and reset it like Jake had explained while he made them, glad she'd forced herself to focus instead of getting distracted by his strong fingers as they deftly wove and knotted the cord.

Ten minutes later, she floated back to the cabin with three rabbits hanging from her hands. The day had gotten brighter, though the sky showed the first signs of sunset. They were getting out of there alive, and she had a plan.

She swung the door open with a triumphant flair. Jake spun from the opposite side of the cabin where he

leaned his head against the log wall. She held in her satis-
fied grin as his jaw dropped.

She tossed the rabbits into the center of the cabin.
"You get those. I'm making a signal."

"Chloe, wait." His call picked up her pace as she
closed the door.

"Can't. Gotta make this before I lose the light." She
cringed at her rudeness and almost turned back.

She couldn't handle his awkward apology or, worse,
his reasons for them to not be together. The reasons were
many. Hadn't she listed them repeatedly in her head
through the years? No. She'd do what she did best, avoid
the issue. She nodded with determination as she gathered
pine branches from the trees Jake had downed and
headed across the hard-packed snow the avalanche had
left. Eventually, her heart would fall in line with her
mind's logic.

JAKE HIT his head against the log wall as Chloe's footsteps retreated. Her red eyes and the dried streaks down
her cheek said he'd made her cry. He wanted to punch
himself in the face. Why had he said those words? He
scoffed at himself. He knew why. Because he was not
only a coward but also a jerk.

He hobbled over to the rabbits and sat down. She'd
gotten three of them. These could feed her for a couple of
days. When the meat was gone, he could make broth out
of the bones. The vice that had clamped around his chest,

and squeezed until he thought he'd die, loosened a fraction.

Ten minutes later, he had the rabbits skinned and gutted. Wild hare didn't have a ton of meat, especially in the dead of winter, but between the organs, muscles, and bones, he knew he could get Chloe some necessary calories she desperately needed.

He sliced up the hearts and put them in water to boil. He'd have her start with that, then he'd roast one of the rabbits whole. He didn't want to make her sicker, so starting slow would be best. If only he had a proper spit, one that wouldn't burn up and drop the rabbit in the fire. His eyes fell on his prosthetic and a bitter smile stretched across his face.

Ripping and prying, he stripped the piece down to the titanium rod that ran through the middle. The fireplace was small and rough enough that he could set the metal on rocks along the inside of the chimney. It positioned the meat in the perfect spot for roasting.

He placed the other two rabbits and edible organs in a plastic storage bag and placed that within a watertight bag. He hoped the two layers would keep any animals away from it. Now if he could find a way to hang it outside on the cabin, they'd be set.

He pulled on his coat and hopped to the door. His heart caught at the sight before him, and he leaned on the doorframe so he didn't buckle. The sunset painted the snow-covered landscape in oranges, purples, and pinks from the bottom of the valley to the tip of the mountains. Chloe had hauled a pile of pine limbs into the open area far enough that a passing plane wouldn't miss it in the trees. Now she worked at laying them out to spell SOS.

He pulled the door closed and leaned against the cabin. She didn't need him, not really. Look at how well she'd taken care of herself so far. He just caused her more work and heartache. Sure, if they lived normal lives, he could probably be enough for her, especially if his nightmares were under control. But she lived an extraordinary life. What if someone tried to attack her and his leg failed again? His dream came rushing back. The sounds of her screams when he couldn't get to her sent ice sliding down his spine. Could he risk that becoming reality?

"Do you think it will work?" Chloe's yell brought his focus back.

She bent over, her hands resting on her thighs as she tried to catch her breath.

"Yeah. It's great. Come inside. I have dinner cooking." He straightened, his hair catching on something and yanking it out.

A bent piece of metal stuck out of the cabin wall. Perfect. He hung the bag of meat on it as Chloe stomped up to the door.

"That was smart to think of that," he offered as she drew close.

She gave him a forced smile and shrugged. "It's probably too small to do any good."

She turned at the door and looked out across the sunset-tinted landscape. Her face turned from contented to dejected. He wanted to snake his arm around her back and pull her close, but he held back.

"I guess we got to watch the sunset after all." Her flat monotone voice broke his heart a little more.

With a sigh, she opened the door and turned away. He followed her into the cabin, closing the beauty out and throwing the cabin into dreary darkness. The wedge his careless words had slammed in between them pinched. If he didn't apologize, the hurt he'd created would continue to wedge space between them. But would she even accept an apology?

"Wow. It smells good." Chloe pulled off her winter gear and hung it on the cargo net. "Where'd you get the spit?"

"Had to put my impotent leg to use somehow." He stripped his coat off and tossed it next to the door. The smell of roasting meat made his stomach growl.

Chloe glanced at him, her eyes narrowing. He ignored it and hopped to the hearth. Using a rag and the pliers on his Leatherman knife, he rotated the rabbit. His words he'd said to her replayed in his head, and he cringed, his appetite gone. He couldn't leave it be, though logic told him to.

He pulled the boiling hearts from the fire, using the delay to figure out what he would say. He cut the meat into smaller pieces, stirred half a packet of salt from the MREs in, and set it in front of their nest to cool. He went to his pile of food and grabbed a pack of crackers so she wouldn't gripe about him not eating.

She'd sat in her usual spot, staring into the fire. Instead of her normal spunk and optimism, her shoulders slumped. He couldn't take it.

Plopping down beside her, he fidgeted with his pant

leg. "I'm sorry, Chloe. I didn't mean what I said. I was angry at myself for failing you and ... and scared."

"You know, that's usually when we are most truthful. When emotions are high." Chloe gingerly picked up the pot of meat and water and poured half into her mug. "I'm a hassle. I'll be one until the day I die. Not many want to sign up voluntarily for that."

She went to pour the rest of the soup in his mug, and he stopped her. "That's yours. I still have food."

Her eyes narrowed, and she glanced toward the pile of food. "Shouldn't we save that just in case we don't catch more rabbits?"

"I'll be fine with what I have for tonight. You need this more than me."

She stared into her mug, stirring the contents with the spoon. *Come on, Silva. You can do this.*

He cleared his throat. "You haven't been a hassle, Chloe. You've been amazing through this entire fiasco."

"Jake, you don't have to lie."

"I'm not lying." He cringed at his yell and softened his tone. "I'm not lying."

She glanced up at him, doubt filling her eyes, and he wanted to lean in and kiss her. Shoot. He wasn't doing a very good job at convincing her she should run far away from him.

"But the truth is I can't take care of you like I am." Jake motioned to his leg.

Chloe closed her eyes and shook her head. "You'll get a new one and be right as rain. Me, on the other hand, I don't have a spare body waiting for me at home."

"That's just it. I'll never be right as rain." He turned

the cracker packet over in his hand. "Maybe if you had a calm, boring life, I could make this work. But what if you're attacked by your stalker or some crazed fans get too excited and my leg gets caught again?"

"That could happen to anyone. Anyone protecting me could fall and get injured."

"Yeah, but a simple trip wouldn't keep them down for long." He shook his head, rubbing his hand across his heart. "In fact, this entire situation has told me I'm not cut out for this line of work. I put our clients and my brothers in more danger by being there."

She took a deep breath and twisted the mug shaking in her hands. "If you think that, you're nuts. You've chopped enough wood to last for weeks. You single-handedly dragged at least four hundred pounds of supplies through a blizzard—"

"It's not that much."

"You found us food in the middle of nowhere and survived an avalanche."

"I wasn't really in the avalanche."

"Would you stop interrupting me?" Chloe huffed. "In the right situation, anyone can fail. You have a better chance at succeeding, because you know you're not invincible."

"It doesn't feel right giving people false security when one misstep would leave them vulnerable." He moved to check the rabbit, needing to escape her defense of him. Escape the notion that he could stay at the ranch and be a part of his team that meant so much to him.

"I guess that's something you'll have to figure out

then." The clink of her spoon on the metal mug reached his ears.

He didn't turn as the sound of her sipping her soup filled the cabin but, rather, leaned against the rugged hearth and stared into the flames. He couldn't let her strained words change his mind. He didn't trust himself, not now, maybe never. When his leg failed again, the consequences could be deadly.

EIGHTEEN

Chloe curled in on herself as she listened to Jake roll over in his sleeping bag on the other side of the cabin. The evening had been tense, and she had inhaled her rabbit hearts, thinking it was a fitting meal when her own heart shriveled in her chest. When she finished, she'd curled into her sleeping bag without saying another word.

She'd pretended to sleep, hoping Jake would snuggle up beside her, but knowing it was futile. When he'd grabbed his bed and moved to the farthest open space in the cabin, her shattered heart froze solid in her chest like the hard-packed snow of the avalanche. She knew she wasn't worth the hassle. Hadn't her parents' own flippancy concerning her taught her that? It was better that she found out now instead of becoming completely entangled with him. If she kept telling herself that, maybe she'd eventually believe it.

He moaned and drew her attention to him across the room. His eyes connected to hers and his body froze. Her breath caught with the emotion in his eyes. Pain? Maybe.

Regret? Most likely. Even her parents regretted having her. Chloe closed her eyes. That was harsh and probably not true.

She couldn't handle the tension. "Ja—"

"Shh." His harsh tone caused her to pinch her mouth shut. "Do you hear that?"

Chloe sat up and cocked her head to the side. A faint thumping noise sounded behind the chirping of the birds. A jolt of excitement raced through her body, rushing the fatigue away.

She turned and smiled at Jake. He rubbed the back of his neck where he sat on the other side of the cabin. "Is that—"

"Helicopter." Jake nodded, his voice strained.

"We're saved," she whispered.

He rubbed his hand across his forehead and swallowed. "Yep."

Her energy hiked, and she had to go see. She scrambled, kicking the sleeping bag that had twisted and bound her legs during the night away from her. She slipped on the snow pants, pulled on her boots, and grabbed her coat as she raced out the door.

Barely stopping to slip on the snowshoes she'd propped against the outside of the cabin, she ran across the top of the snow to her signal, bracing her hands on her knees as she caught her breath. The sun hadn't reached the valley floor, only highlighting the craggy mountain tops with bright morning light. Would they be able to see her? She glanced at the limbs lined up around her and wondered if she should pile them up to light a bonfire.

The wind whistled through the valley, blowing its frigid fingers into her coat. She shivered and quickly zipped it up. She turned in a slow circle, scanning the air for the helicopter. The thumps of the rotors echoed from every direction. Why couldn't she see it?

The icy air and frantic run made her throat raw. The wood smoke and fresh pine scents calmed her racing heart. Her scan halted on Jake who leaned against the cabin watching her.

"Where are they?" She hated the trepidation that pushed the joy from her.

"Sound travels funny in mountains like these." He surveyed the ridges behind her. "They could be miles away or right over the peak. It might be a while before they find us."

Her shoulders slumped as she peered back into the sky. "Should I pile all these limbs up and light a bonfire?"

His lips tweaked up in one corner. "What are you going to use as a starter? We're all out of spare undergarments."

Their gazes connected, the tension leaving his face as a genuine smile tipped the other side of his mouth up. Her face heated in embarrassment, but the goosebumps that rose on her skin wasn't from the cold. Could she figure out a way to keep what she'd found while stranded in the Colorado wilds? Figure out a way to not be such a burden?

His comment about starting her own music label sprang to her mind. Could she do that? Maybe find a following on YouTube, doing fewer live concerts. That appealed to her more than she cared to admit. The constant travel had taxed her body. She'd hate to give up concerts completely, but maybe she could pick only the ones she wanted instead of all the ones offered.

As the sun crested the peak and shone its brilliance on Jake, her inner scramble stuttered to a halt. It wasn't her schedule he'd been opposed to. There was nothing she could do about her health. Her bum genetics weren't leaving her anytime soon. In fact, it could get worse as years went by. She blinked rapidly as her eyes filled and nose stung.

Jake glanced down at his leg as he scratched his thigh, breaking their connection. "Why don't you come in and eat something? We could be waiting a long time before they get to us."

Her shoulders dropped, and she didn't have the will to push them back up. She should be hungry, but the thought of eating made her nauseous. Maybe she'd just sit on the porch and finish watching the day begin.

The choppy sounds of blades spinning through the air thundered into the valley. She turned as a helicopter crested the mountain, the sun haloing it like a metal guardian angel. She let out a loud whoop, jumping up and down and waving her arms like a madwoman.

She glanced back to Jake. The serious set of his face chilled the warmth that had spread through her at the sight of their rescue. He didn't look at her, just focused on the approaching helicopter with dull eyes. His hand opened and closed at his side and his shoulders hung low. Would he be in trouble for wrecking the plane? Was he even a little sorry their time together was ending, or was he just glad to be rid of her?

She turned back toward their rescuers as the helicopter descended, glad she didn't have to make Jake uncomfortable anymore. Relief from the worry and pain hit her, and the tension that had held her muscles taut over the last four days rushed from her. Her knees buckled, and she sank to the snow.

Lifting a shaky hand to cover her eyes from the violent wind pelting her with snow, silent sobs welled up and shook her shoulders. They were saved. Why didn't she feel more happiness? Why did her stomach twist? She peeked back at Jake. He still didn't look at her. She hadn't felt this amount of despair since her time in the hospital.

"Chloe!" Rafe's call whipped her head to the helicopter that was landing.

Rafe jumped from the open door before the bird touched down, hitting the hard-packed snow and tucking into a roll. She brought her trembling fingers to her lips and burst out laughing. He came out of his impressive dismount and stood with ease. His snowshoes kicked a trail of snow into the air as he ran across the surface toward her.

"Chloe, are you all right?" Rafe asked, concern creasing his forehead.

She nodded, her throat too thick to speak.

He kneeled down in front of her and pulled her into a bear hug. "Thank God you're alive." He squeezed her tighter. "Piper would've killed me if I didn't come home with you."

"Thanks for finding us."

"We would've been here sooner, but the weather

didn't cooperate." A tall man with short dark hair and piercing blue eyes came up behind Rafe. "I'm Zeke Greene. Nice to finally meet you."

Chloe smiled and nodded.

"Where's Jake?" Zeke scanned the area, his eyes going wide. "Where's my plane?"

She looked back at the open door of the cabin. "Jake must be inside. An avalanche buried your plane."

"What?" Zeke turned around and held his hand to his forehead as he searched the valley.

"It was my fault, really. I pointed this area out, not realizing it was an avalanche shoot." Chloe's words rushed out, hoping to turn any blame on herself.

"I could care less about the plane." Zeke glanced down at her. "You two have been through it, haven't you?"

Chloe nodded. She squeezed her eyes to hold the tears in. They had been through it, but they were alive.

"Let's get home." Rafe snaked his hand around her back and helped her stand.

Zeke placed a hand on her shoulder and strode toward the cabin. She longed to see Jake, to see his reactions, but he stayed inside. Rafe pulled on her, and her knees buckled with the first step.

"Here we go." Rafe swung her into his arms like she weighed as much as a child. "Land sakes, woman. You're nothing but skin and bones. We need to get some meat on you."

"Yeah, well, any meat I had melted away with little to eat but meal replacement bars and bad coffee," she tried to joke.

Rafe sobered. "Piper worried about that. When we told her the plane had provisions, she demanded I opened some we had at the ranch so she could see what you had." Rafe shook his head. "When did she get so bossy?"

Chloe snorted a laugh. "She's always been bossy, just in a quiet way where you don't realize she's bossing you." She laid her head on his shoulder when it became too heavy to hold up. "How is she?"

"Beautiful." Rafe smiled when Chloe lifted her head and peered at him. "Why did I never notice that before?"

"Because you're an idiot."

"Yeah, probably right." Rafe sighed. "She's been a worried mess."

Rafe set Chloe in the helicopter door and patted her leg like a child. "Now you sit tight while we gather everything up." He gave her knee a squeeze. "I'm glad you're fine."

"Me, too." She smiled despite the lie. She wasn't sure how she was. "We have some snares out behind the cabin."

Rafe waved and took off toward the woods. Chloe lifted her feet that weighed a ton and pulled her snowshoes off, tucking them under the seat as Zeke emerged from the cabin carrying one of the packs. She said hello to the pilot as he waved at her, then scooted back and climbed into the seat on the far side of the interior. How was it that she hadn't felt this tired the entire time they were stranded? Leaning against the window, she watched as Zeke and Rafe brought the supplies from the cabin.

After a couple of trips, Rafe climbed in and began

strapping the packs to the floor. She leaned forward to help, but he waved her off. She didn't want to admit how relieved that made her. She hardly had the energy to keep her head up, which was weird since she'd had plenty of energy before.

Her heart picked up as Zeke came out with Jake under his shoulder. Jake met her gaze, then quickly lowered his head. Her heart stuttered. Was he embarrassed that he needed help?

When they made it to the helicopter, Jake placed his hands on the floor and hoisted himself inside. Chloe stared at him as he hopped around the packs and sank into the seat across from her. Her vision blurred and heat rose up her chest. She wouldn't cry—not here. She caught Rafe's eyebrows draw close together when he glanced from her to Jake. Rafe shook his head, muttering something she couldn't hear with the engine powering up.

Rafe plopped next to her and draped his arm across her shoulder. "You okay?"

She nodded. Jake's distance would not turn her into a blubbering mess. She stared out of the window at the snow-covered landscape as the helicopter lifted into the air. She blamed the dropping sensation in her stomach on the takeoff rather than the freeze-out she was getting from Jake.

NINETEEN

Jake refused to look at Chloe—at least straight on. She stayed glued in his peripheral, despite his effort to ignore her. Every time her shoulders would slump, a stab would go straight to his heart.

Jerk.

Rafe had hit that nail on the head when he had muttered that Jake was an idiot. It couldn't be helped. He had to sever this tie that had wrapped around them, so she could find someone who could really take care of her. Two broken people in a relationship just wasn't healthy. He couldn't be the weak link holding her down from her dreams.

Couldn't watch himself fall short over and over again.

So he pretended to stare out the window while he watched the woman of his dreams gather her strength back up around her.

"We'll be landing at Valley View Hospital in about five minutes," Zeke announced over the headset.

"Hospital? I don't need to go to a hospital." The panic in Chloe's voice nearly broke his heart.

She'd told him, during one of their many talks, how much she hated hospitals. It was something they both had in common. She caught his gaze, her eyes begging him to say something.

He clenched his jaw and turned back to the window. "Good. She needs to be checked out."

Her hands twisted in her lap. He could feel the hot anger shooting across the packs at him from her. From Rafe and Zeke as well.

The helicopter touched down, and he stayed in his seat as Rafe helped Chloe into a waiting wheelchair. Piper stood just inside the glass doors to the hospital, her hands wringing in front of her.

"Take the helicopter to my ranch." Zeke patted the pilot on the shoulder. "I'll have someone waiting to unload this gear."

"Copy that." The pilot nodded.

Jake grabbed Zeke's arm before he could jump out. "I'm heading back with the helicopter."

"You need to be checked out too." Zeke's eyebrows pinched.

Jake shook his head. "Nah, I ate well. Drank enough. Nothing's injured." *Except my pride.* He kept that last part to himself.

"What about Chloe?"

"What about her?" Jake averted his gaze to the red-rocked mountain behind the hospital.

"I don't know, maybe the fact that there's so much

emotion bouncing between the two of you there was hardly room for me and Rafe in the helo?"

"It's nothing."

"Really?" Zeke's tone called Jake out.

Jake turned to Zeke, meeting his steely gaze, forcing his face to remain emotionless.

Praying his friend would drop it and let him go.

"Really," Jake choked out.

Zeke stared Jake down. When Jake thought he would cave, Zeke snorted and shook his head.

"Whatever." He climbed out of the helicopter and turned back. "You've always been a horrible liar, Jake."

With that, he slammed the door and took off for the hospital. The sinking of Jake's stomach as the helicopter took off reminded him he hadn't eaten breakfast yet. He didn't have an appetite, anyway. Probably never would again.

Sosimo and June waited at the ranch's landing strip when the helicopter touched down. Of course a happy couple would be waiting for his return. Another turn of the knife jabbed his heart to make sure he bled out completely.

June stepped up, her bottom lip pulled between her teeth as she handed him one of his prosthetics from his cabin. "Zeke called and said the other one was busted."

"Yeah. Thanks." Jake slipped the limb on, taking a deep breath.

"I'd like to talk to you about what happened, see how it failed." Her eyes widened, and she quickly fumbled with her words. "That is ... I mean, when you are up to it."

"Cariña, why don't you let Jake get out of the helo?" Sosimo wrapped his arm over her shoulder and stepped back.

"Right, of course." June's fair skin blushed to match her red hair.

Jake eased out of the helicopter, testing his weight on his leg. He half expected it to buckle from underneath him. June launched herself toward him, wrapping him in a tight hug.

"I'm so glad you're safe." She sniffed and squeezed harder. "We've been so worried."

His throat felt thick, and he sucked the inside of his cheeks between his teeth to keep his emotions under control. Sosimo shook his head, throwing his hands up in an I-give-up motion. Jake patted her on the back. She pulled away, wiping her hands across her wet cheeks, and tucked into Sosimo's side.

"We brought your truck down. The keys are in it." Sosimo pointed his thumb to Jake's Toyota. "Head on over to your place. You need a shower." Sosimo scrunched his nose. "You're making my eyes water."

June gasped and smacked Sosimo on the chest. "Don't be rude."

Jake forced a chuckle. "Thanks."

Finally, he could escape.

Could hide himself from the world.

He waved his hand and trudged his way to his truck. When he pulled up to his cabin, he groaned. Samantha's vehicle was parked in front. He didn't want to visit with Zeke's wife. He wanted to take a shower, then try to not think about how Chloe was doing at the hospital.

As he turned the ignition off and stepped out of the vehicle, the door to his place swung open. A gleeful squeal preceded Eva as she barreled out of the cabin. Her skinny legs moved so quickly that her curly pigtails flew straight out behind her. Jake barely had time to brace himself before she jumped into his arms and wrapped her limbs around him.

"Oh, Jake, I've missed you so much." Her tiny voice caught, and she buried her face deeper into his neck.

Jake squeezed his teary eyes shut and cleared his throat. "I missed you too."

"Everyone's been so worried, but I knew you'd be okay." Eva put her small hands on his cheeks. "You're so brave and strong. I knew nothing would keep you away for long. Plus, I was praying really hard. God always listens when you pray, so I knew you'd be okay."

Man, she was killing him. "Thanks, honey."

"Rafe said you were protecting a princess. Did you save her?" Eva chatted while he carried her to the cabin.

His energy seemed to leak right out of him. "Nope. She saved me."

Eva's bright blue eyes grew wide above her freckled cheeks. "She did."

"Yep."

"Wow." Eva looked out over the meadow in awe. "I want to be a princess like her."

"She's special, that's for sure." He needed to stop talking about Chloe before he lost his resolve and drove down to the hospital.

She'd probably forgive him if he groveled well enough. He scoffed. She'd forgive him even if he didn't.

That's the type of person she was. He had to stop thinking about her. He still couldn't keep her.

He stepped into the house, and a savory smell set his stomach to grumbling. Maybe he could eat something. Sam wiped off the counter and gave him a smile.

"Eva, we're going to let Jake rest." Sam stopped in front of him and cringed as she scanned him up and down. "And shower. You look horrible."

Jake laughed, setting Eva on the ground. "I feel horrible."

Sam sobered. "Are you all right? We've been so worried."

"Yeah, I'm fine." Jake nodded and rubbed the back of his neck.

Sam stepped up and gave him a quick hug. "I'm glad." She sniffed and stepped back. "I have stew on the stove for you."

"I made you your favorite peanut butter cookies." Eva hugged his leg.

"Thanks."

"Come up to the main house when you're ready." Sam placed a hand on his shoulder, then grabbed Eva's arm. "Come on, sweetie. Let's go bake some more treats."

"Yeah!" Eva took off for the door. "See you soon, Jake."

The door clicked, and familiar silence surrounded him. Why did it now feel stifling when before it had been his companion? He shook it off and got in the shower. When thirty minutes of steaming water and a bowl of thick stew didn't loosen the weight of loneliness, a sinking feeling hardened his gut. Without Chloe, life threatened to be a barren tomb.

CHLOE STARED out the hospital window as snow fell lazily outside. The low, gray clouds matched her dreary emotions. When Jake hadn't followed her in, her heart had sunk. As the hours passed and he didn't show, her heart shriveled and died. It surprised her that the monitor next to her continued to beep at a steady rhythm.

Piper's phone rang, causing Chloe to jump. Piper's forehead scrunched as she looked at the phone number and excused herself into the hall. Rafe's gaze lingered on the door before turning back to Chloe.

"Did you get any more information on my stalker?" Chloe asked Rafe now that Piper had slipped out of the room.

"Yeah." He looked back out the door.

"And?"

"It appears the dude is stalking Piper, not you."

Her eyes darted to the hall where Piper chatted on the phone. The lunch the hospital had served curdled in Chloe's stomach. She sat up and swung her legs over the edge of the bed.

"Whoa, Snappy. You aren't cleared to leave yet." Rafe held his hands in front of him to calm her down.

"We have to leave. Go hide until we can find this guy."

"Chloe, I'm not about to let anything happen to Piper." His tone was one she'd never heard before. "We have it under control. You don't need to worry. I promise."

She tucked her legs back in the bed. How could she have been so blind? She pulled her knees to her chest and laid her head on her knees. If only Jake was here to help her talk this through. She scoffed at herself. She needed to purge thoughts like that out of her head. It was obvious Jake was done with her.

Rafe cleared his throat. "I'm sorry, Chlo."

Chloe shook the doldrums from her unsettled brain. "What?"

"Jake, the numskull." Rafe rolled his eyes. "I'm sorry he hasn't come by."

Had her thoughts been broadcasted so clearly? She pushed her lips up, though she feared it was more a grimace than a smile. "It's okay."

"What happened between you two?"

"We ... I—"

"Chloe." Piper came rushing in with her hand over her phone. "*Hello, America* wants you to come out for an interview."

"What?" Chloe sat up, her heart jumpstarting.

"They picked up the story somehow. They know you won't be able to make it for tomorrow's show, but they want to interview you the next morning." Piper's excitement mirrored Chloe's own.

This could be it. This could be the break they needed. She chewed on her bottom lip.

"Tell them I can come for the interview, give them all the juicy plane crash details, but I'd like to perform a song with my band as well." Chloe's gut twisted at the demand. Would they accept or was she throwing her chance to being discovered out the window?

Piper relayed the message in a much more diplomatic way. She truly was amazing at this stuff. Her smile beamed from her face as she gave Chloe a thumbs up. Chloe kicked her legs, and they both did a happy dance while Piper finished the call.

Piper hung up, and Rafe roared, wrapping Piper in a hug and spinning her around. He set her down and pushed her hair behind her ear. The touching motion caused Chloe's eyes to tear, so she picked at her hospital blanket to avert her gaze.

"Excuse me." A nurse peeked her head in the room. "I'm going to have to ask you to keep it down in here."

"Sorry." Piper stepped away from Rafe, her hand rubbing her cheek where Rafe had touched.

Derrick, a man Zeke had said would help Rafe, stepped into the room. He had said little to her, instead kept watch while Rafe stayed close.

"What's up?" His deep, steady voice was mellow and unaffected by the excitement pinging through the room.

"We need to head to New York." Rafe clapped Derrick on the shoulder.

His dark eyebrow cocked. "Okay."

Piper sat on the end of the hospital bed. "Chloe's going to be interviewed on *Hello, America*." She scrunched her forehead. "Is it too late to charter a private airplane to fly us all out there?"

"That shouldn't be a problem." Rafe pulled out his phone.

Derrick went back into the hall to keep guard,

putting his phone to his ear. Piper called Chet and told him to get the band packed and ready to go. They'd all come to see Chloe shortly after she'd arrived. They'd driven to Glenwood to help however they could with the search and rescue. It had been sweet of her bandmates to want to help.

Chloe turned her gaze out the window as the chatter blended together. She wanted the excitement to overtake the sadness. Wanted the joy this opportunity gave them to bubble up and drown her in giddiness. It didn't, though—just kind of fizzled in the bottom of her.

Maybe it was better this way. Putting distance between her and Jake would give her the space needed. It would also keep her from doing something royally stupid like catch an Uber to Jake's and demand he love her as much as she did him. Maybe once she got over the hurt and anger, she'd have the strength to fight for him. Right now, she barely had the strength to hold her tears in that threatened to fall. She reached for the nurse's call button, determined to get out of this hospital and Colorado as fast as possible.

TWENTY

Jake huffed and tossed the wood planer onto the worktable. He grabbed the board he'd been working on and tossed it into the pile with the others he'd destroyed. He had thought working on his cabin would help him keep his mind off the fact that Chloe had left. It hadn't taken her long to get over whatever it was they had and get back to what drove her.

Jake had protested when Zeke had come by to tell him. Jake had argued she needed to stay in the hospital longer, make sure everything checked out. The look Zeke had given Jake told him Zeke didn't buy that load of goat dung. Now, Jake wasn't just a jerk, but he was a selfish jerk. He'd almost caved when Zeke asked if Jake wanted to go to New York with Chloe, make sure she stayed safe.

He stomped out of the spare room he'd turned into a workroom. Maybe he should just go to bed. He shook his head. With how amped up he was, that would only bring more nightmares.

He slumped in his armchair, the fire the only light in

the room. His bearded dragon, Rex, touched his nose to the glass of his tank and cocked his head.

"At least I still have you." Jake scoffed as he reached into the tank and pulled the lizard out.

Rex clung to Jake's forearm as he rubbed his finger down the lizard's back. The rhythmic motion normally settled him, but not tonight. He stared out the window as the snow fell lazily against the inky night.

"She's amazing, Rex. You would've really liked her. She sings like an angel, her voice soothing the beast that rages inside me." His habit of talking with the dragon didn't bother him as much as it had when he first got Rex. Sometimes Jake needed to talk things through, and Rex was a superb listener.

"She got all excited when I told her about you, said she'd always wanted a pet lizard or boa or something. Imagine that, a prissy rich girl wanting a reptile for a pet." He rubbed the back of his neck. "She's not prissy, though. She's tough, has the strength of a fighter, and won't back down."

Unlike him.

He pressed his thumb and finger against his eyes, then pinched the ridge of his nose, trying to fight the memory of her breaching his borders and kicking in the door to his heart. His wounds hadn't bothered her. He closed his eyes and could almost feel her small fingers massaging his leg. His skin had zipped with every rub. His leg hadn't felt that good since his surgeries.

She'd even woken him from his dreams without him freaking out. He rubbed his lips with the back of his knuckle, then growled low. Thinking about kissing her wouldn't help him at all. He put Rex back in his tank and stalked to the kitchen. Grabbing a cookie from Eva off the plate, he bit it in half and chewed his frustration out.

Why was he dwelling on this? He'd gotten what he wanted. She had moved on, and Rafe and Derrick would keep her safe.

So why did it feel like he was making the biggest mistake of his life?

The cookie turned to sawdust in his mouth. His shoulders slumped as he tossed the rest of the cookie on the plate. He had done the right thing in pushing her away, hadn't he? He shook his head. He hadn't gone wrong there.

Falling in love with her had been the mistake.

One he'd regret the rest of his life.

"UNCLE JAKE." Loud banging opened Jake's eyes to bright sun filtering through his living room window.

He rolled his neck. He hated when he fell asleep on the recliner. Gave him a headache the rest of the day.

The pounding intensified and made him cringe. "Uncle Jake, are you in there?"

"Come on in, Eva." Jake stretched, trying to get the kinks out.

Eva opened the door with a bang and ran in, only to skid to a stop and run back to the door. She slammed it—hard—and Jake flinched. He'd have to find the essential oil roller Zeke's stepmom had given him for his headaches.

He braced a split second before Eva jumped onto his lap. "What's got you visiting this early?"

"It's not early, silly." She giggled and shook her head. "It's almost lunchtime."

Jake peered at the clock on the wall. Huh, he'd slept better than he thought.

"I've come to talk some sense into you." She crossed her arms over her chest and put on her serious face.

He'd have had a hard time keeping a straight face if her words didn't fill him with dread.

"Huh."

"Uncle Jake, why'd you let Miss Chloe go?"

Yep, dread was right. "She's better off without me."

Eva shook her head, her curls swinging with the enthusiastic motion. "Nah-uh. She's not. That's not what Uncle Rafe said."

"What do you mean?"

"He said she's sad, that she's hardly eating and all the light has gone out of her."

Jake stood fast, almost dumping Eva on the floor. He set her on her feet and paced to the kitchen.

"Why isn't she eating? She practically starved while we were stuck in that cabin." He speared his fingers through his tangled hair.

"Rafe says she's hardly come out of her room in the suite they're staying in. Piper's worried she going to mess up the interview." Eva grabbed his hand and gazed up at him with watery blue eyes. "They say it's your fault. That you're a numskull. Are you a numskull, Uncle Jake?"

His chin drooped to his chest. The thought of Chloe hurting weighed heavy on his shoulders.

"Yeah, sweetheart, I'm a numskull."

"Then stop being one and go rescue her." Eva stomped her foot and placed her hands on her hips.

He wanted to. His heart raced with the thought of going to her. Yet, fear wound its icy fingers through his gut and squeezed.

"It's not that easy." Jake leaned against the counter.

"Yes, it is." Eva crossed her arms. For a four-year-old, she was persistent. "You just fly to New York and apologize."

"Eva, I can't protect her. Can't take care of her the way I need to."

"So that's what this is all about?" Zeke's concerned voice turned Jake's head to the door.

"Daddy!" Eva ran to Zeke and threw her arms around his waist, Jake's heart clenching with the thought that he'd never have a child do that. "I tried, Daddy, but he's still being a numskull."

Zeke pulled on a curl, a soft smile on his face. "Why don't you go wait in the car and let me have a shot at him?"

"Knock some dollars in him." Eva's serious tone was back.

Jake snorted at another of Eva's messed up phrases.

"If I have to, I'll knock a lot of sense into him."

"Good." She hugged her dad and turned to Jake. "Uncle Jake, you listen and obey Daddy, okay? And brush your teeth. You can't rescue your princess with stinky breath."

Jake and Zeke burst out laughing. Eva dashed out the door with as much energy as when she'd arrived. Jake turned away from the door to make coffee. He had to do something. Couldn't just stand there and let Zeke wear down his already thinning defenses.

"So you think you can't keep her safe?" Zeke's tone had turned back to his Army sergeant voice.

Jake grunted.

"So what do you call what you did out on that mountain?"

"Almost getting her killed. That's what I call it." Jake slammed the lid down on the coffee pod and jammed the button.

"That's not what she said. She said you were amazing."

Jake snorted and turned around, leaning his back against the counter.

"Seriously, man. And I'd have to agree with her."

"I almost got her killed. Couldn't do a single thing after my prosthetic broke."

"She said you chopped that pile of firewood after the avalanche."

"Which she had to carry in after she'd practically starved for four days," Jake yelled.

The coffee beeped, and he spun to keep from punching something.

"Seems to me, she's the type who'd rather help than stand helplessly to the side." Zeke's quiet tone irked Jake, mostly because Zeke was right.

"Zeke, man, I can't. I'm a liability to her, and to you and the company for that matter."

"That's a load of bull." Zeke rounded the counter and pushed Jake's shoulder to get him to face him. "You are one of the best men I know. You train harder and longer than any of us. Your leg doesn't put you at a disadvantage. If anything, it's made you a stronger person."

"Now who's shoveling it?" Jake jerked his shoulder away. "My leg slips or breaks, and anyone I'm protecting is left vulnerable."

"That could happen to any of us. There's always been that risk. Always."

"Yeah, right," Jake scoffed.

"You *are* a numskull. You're going to throw away the love of an amazing woman, a survivor just like you, and the possibility of a family, over an issue that's not even a problem." Zeke's voice dripped with the disgust Jake felt inside.

Jake closed his eyes and shook his head. "It's more than the leg. I have nightmares. I literally threw her across the cabin when she tried to wake me. I can't—" He swallowed the tears that clogged his throat. "I can't even keep her safe from me."

"You're not alone in that." Zeke placed his hand on Jake's shoulder and squeezed. "I have nightmares too." He rubbed his hand through his short, dark brown hair. "I accidentally hit Sam clear off the bed one night."

Jake's stomach flipped at the thought. "No."

"Yeah. When I realized what I'd done, I freaked. Started bawling like a baby." He cringed. "Told her I was sleeping on the couch so I couldn't hurt her." He chuckled and shook his head. "She told me to stop being an idiot. That she hated sleeping on the couch, and since she wouldn't sleep without me, I wasn't leaving the bed."

"But Chloe is so fragile."

"I won't tell her you said that." Zeke cocked his eyebrow.

"I'm serious. Her body is weak from celiac." Jake wished Zeke wasn't blocking the only escape from the small U-shaped kitchen.

"You love her." Zeke shook his head and glared when Jake opened his mouth to dispute it. "You can't hide it from me. And she loves you. Whatever happened up on that mountain bound you together."

"Nothing untoward happened. I made sure we didn't go past kissing," Jake quickly explained.

"I didn't mean that." Zeke rolled his eyes. "Don't be a fool and let your pride lose her. She's the future you always prattled on and on about."

"I don't prattle, and that was before." Jake crossed his arms, squeezing the hope that expanded in his chest.

"Okay, droned. Droned on and on about the wife you'd find that was perfect for you." Zeke stepped around the counter. "She's miserable. You're miserable. It's not too late to grab hold of that happily ever after Eva's so nuts about. You've never been a coward, Jake, so stop acting like one."

Zeke's words pinched. He'd known all along that he couldn't live without Chloe, but the idea of not being enough for a girl like her had been overwhelming. Jake rubbed his hand across his chest. Zeke was right. He was crazy to let her go.

Warmth spread and scattered his cold fear at the thought of seeing her again. He had to get to New York. Chloe questioning him about not seeing how people really saw him came to mind. If he was wrong about how others reacted to him, he couldn't trust his perspective on this either. A slow smile grew. He'd just have to trust Chloe and her insistence that they would work.

He took off toward his room. "I need to get to New York."

"Finally." Zeke threw his arms up. "I was starting to worry I'd have to knock you out and throw you on the plane."

"Plane?" Jake called from his room as he threw clothes into a bag.

"I have a jet waiting for you. You'll be in New York in under four hours if you hurry."

Jake rushed from his room. "I'm ready."

Zeke shook his head. "Man, you need to brush your teeth, maybe dress in something other than sweats. You're going to woo your future wife. You can't do that looking like you just rolled out of bed."

Jake looked down and cringed at his sawdust-spotted sweats and paint-splattered t-shirt. "Right. Tell the pilot I'll be there in thirty, and he better be ready to go, or I'm taking his plane and flying myself."

Zeke threw his head back and laughed. "I'll be sure to tell him. I'll throw in that the last plane you flew, you crashed. That might get him moving."

Jake pulled off his shirt as he headed for the shower. He felt lighter than he had in days, probably years. He had four hours to come up with a plan, something that told Chloe he wasn't going anywhere. He'd also have a lot of groveling to do. And kissing, lots and lots of kissing.

TWENTY-ONE

Chloe paced in front of the fireplace in her and Piper's room at The Plaza in New York City. Her father had insisted that she be comfortable after her ordeal and had reserved the Royal Suite. His quiet comment about how much he knew she loved *Eloise* had stifled her objection to the opulence. Now, she was grateful for the semi-privacy the suite provided.

She'd fallen asleep the night before, the instant they had gotten there, then she'd isolated herself from the others. Her appetite was nil, which surprised her. All the days they'd been stranded, she'd had to work hard not to obsess over food. Now, she just ate because she knew she had to.

She simply wanted to be alone. Wanted time to recollect all that had happened and work out whether what she and Jake had found was all in her head or not. After hours of poring over her memories, she understood without a doubt that Jake loved her. She stopped and scrunched her forehead—or at least cared for her.

She paced the room again and stood in front of the window that overlooked Fifth Avenue. The fading sun painted the sky like juicy tangerines and grapefruit flesh nestled into deep, dark plums. Hmm, maybe she was hungry. She shook off the thought. Decisions had to be made before she could stop to think about eating.

The honking of horns and cacophony of traffic filtered through the glass. She missed the quiet. Missed the two-tone *dee-dee-dee* call as chickadees flew from tree to tree. Missed the sound of snow falling from branches with a thump.

But mostly, she missed the crackling of the fire. The slight rasp of Jake's calloused fingers as they made slow circles on her arm. The quiet conversations that filled her heart more than any concert crowd ever had.

Lights blinked on throughout the city, but she barely saw them. Her reflection stared at her, daring her to take a real risk. It might cost her the chance to make it big, but she might gain something much more important than fame.

She closed her eyes and saw Jake's vulnerability as he had told her about his hurts. He was worth any risk. She couldn't stay here without knowing for sure. A slow smile built in her reflection. It filled her with calm and confidence.

Turning, she stomped to the door, yelling to the others somewhere in the suite, "We have to leave. I have to get to Colorado now."

Her voice faded, and her feet froze. Jake stood in the living room, his hands twisting in front of him. A door clicked closed, but she couldn't tear her gaze from him.

He cocked his eyebrow. "Colorado?"

His deep voice raised the hairs on her neck and arms. Her words bottled up in her throat, so she nodded.

"Why?" He took a step closer.

"You." Her voice cracked, and she swallowed the emotion from her throat. "I'm going to Colorado for you."

His eyebrows pulled together. "But your interview."

"Doesn't matter." She shook her head and inched forward. "Nothing matters to me as much as you do."

He closed the space in two steps and lifted his hand to her cheek. He was here. Her entire world shifted right on its axis. She closed her eyes and leaned her head into his touch. She had to know. Had he come for her or because of his job?

"Why are you here?" Her voice wasn't more than a whisper as her breath stalled in her chest.

Jake brought his other hand up and cupped her cheek. He trailed his thumb over her lips, his gaze holding hers.

"We seem to have a similar problem. Nothing matters to me but you." He leaned close, his lip brushing hers. "Nothing."

She threw her arms around his neck and kissed him hard. Heat exploded from her chest and left her weightless. He'd come for her. To a city full of people. He wrapped his arms around her and pulled her to him, and she wondered if love could expand so much within her it'd flash out through the windows like all those sci-fi movies.

He put her feet down and leaned his forehead against

hers. "I'm so sorry, Chloe. I was an idiot. Eva called me a numskull. I should've never left you at the hospital."

"Why did you?" She leaned away, keeping her hands on his shoulders.

His fingers flexed against her back, and he cringed. "I was afraid." He closed his eyes, swallowed, then held her gaze with a pained stare. "Scared I couldn't keep you safe. Scared my leg would rip off, and I couldn't save you."

"I'm not worried."

"I am." He sighed. "But I don't want to hide away in my cabin anymore. I want to explore life with you, traveling to hear your voice lace peace within me and keep the overenthusiastic fans away."

Her laugh came out breathless and happy. "I don't even have any overenthusiastic fans. Piper does."

Jake's expression grew serious. "We'll figure out who it is, I promise."

"I know you guys will. Besides, I think Rafe has a vested interest in keeping her protected now, beyond just because she's Davis's sister."

He walked backward, pulling her with him until he sat on the back of the couch. "Chloe, I have little I can offer you, but I can't imagine being away from you again. Wherever you are, New York, Texas, Nashville, and anywhere in between, I want to be right beside you."

Could someone faint from happiness? Chloe blinked her eyes to clear the tears. She didn't want to miss a second of him.

"I think a ranch in Colorado sounds nice, too." Chloe

leaned against him. "Someone once told me I should look into going indie. That sounds mighty appealing."

He smiled, then grew serious. "My entire life I dreamed of following in my family's legacy, serving my country honorably, and having a family to share life with. I thought I'd lost that dream. But then I was assigned to protect you and all that changed."

He moved from the couch, reached into his pocket, and kneeled on his prosthetic knee. Her pulse beat in her throat and her mouth went dry. He twisted the ring in his hands.

"I bought this ring while doing reconnaissance during a mission in Turkey." His ears turned pink, and Chloe smiled. "It's silly, really. What kind of guy buys a ring while on a mission when he doesn't even have a girl-friend? But I saw it and knew it was the one I was supposed to buy." He lifted it up to her. "I buried it in the back of my drawer. I'm surprised I didn't chuck it." He shook his head. "I'm screwing this up."

"No, no you're not." Chloe covered her lips with her fingertips.

"Chloe Rose Fields, you make me want to be brave again. You've brought joy into my gray life and song into my spirit. Will you share this life with me and be my wife?"

"Yes." Her answer caught in her throat. She stepped into him, threaded her hands through his hair, and kissed him. "I love you, Jake Silva, and I can't wait for the adventures life has for us."

He kissed her while he stood, lifting her off her feet. When he set her down, her knees almost collapsed

CRASHING INTO JAKE   185

beneath her. She gasped as he slipped the ring on her finger.

Never had she seen a ring as unique as the one now nestled on her hand. It had a diamond inset in the middle surrounded by eight smaller diamonds to form a circle. Connected to that, two rows of curved golden arches created open petals and connected to the gold band.

"It's gorgeous."

"A rose for my rose," Jake whispered against her neck, the touch sending shivers down her back. "I love you, Chloe."

She couldn't stop the tears that streamed down her cheeks as she kissed him. There was no containing joy when it sprung forth. She wasn't sure how long that Kissing Time lasted, but she knew over ten minutes had passed before the others returned and they could share their news.

"WELCOME BACK TO *HELLO, America*. We are so excited to introduce you all to America's next country starlet, Chloe Rose." The perky blonde host turned to Chloe with a million-dollar smile that could blind some-one, making Jake sweat with nerves for Chloe. "Chloe, it's so good of you to join us."

"It's a pleasure to be here, Shelly." Chloe appeared cool as a cucumber, and Jake marveled at how beautiful she was.

She'd fretted all last night, modeling outfit after outfit. He'd thought she looked beautiful in all of them and told her so. When she'd stepped out in the turquoise dress that flared when she twirled, Jake hadn't been able to say a thing, his eyes bugging out and his mouth gaping open. Rafe had slapped him on the back and claimed they had found the outfit. She'd blushed prettily as she had given him a kiss and went back to her room to change.

Now, he wondered if she should've worn a different outfit. She was stunning and glowed with happiness. She'd have men clamoring to her the instant the interview finished. Jake clenched his teeth.

"Chloe, we hear you had quite the ordeal last week. Could you tell us about it?" The co-host, Brian, leaned forward in his seat, concern crinkling his forehead.

"It was an adventure for sure, Brian." Chloe animatedly described the plane crash and what followed, her arms waving with dramatic flair.

His ears heated as she painted him in a light much more heroic than necessary. He pulled his earlobe and shifted on his feet.

Rafe leaned close. "Man, I think I want to marry you after that story."

Jake elbowed him in the side. "Shh."

"Now, Chloe, just between you and me." Shelly leaned in close with her hand on her face like she was sharing a secret. "It seems like this Jake and you shared more than just a few stranded days in the wilderness, if you know what I mean?"

Chloe smiled, looked at the giggling audience, then glanced at Jake. Her smile broadened before she turned back to the hosts.

"There is. We're getting married." She held up her hand and wiggled her fingers.

"Oh, how exciting." Brian shielded his eyes with his cue cards. "Is your fiancé here with you?"

"Yep." Chloe pointed, and Jake's heart thundered in his chest.

"Come on over here, Jake." Shelly waved her hand for Jake to join Chloe.

Rafe pushed Jake's back and propelled him forward. His hands had never sweated like they did at that point, and he tried to wipe them inconspicuously on his pants. The scar on his cheek itched. This was a mistake. He made it to the stage, shook the hosts' hands, gave Chloe a peck on the cheek, then took the tall chair next to her. He forced his mouth to smile and his leg not to bounce.

Shelly fanned herself with her cards. "Whew. If this is what rescuers look like, sign me up!"

Jake's neck heated as Chloe glanced at him. She bit her lip, and her eyes sparkled in amusement.

Brian rolled his eyes dramatically. "Shelly, you realize that means a plane crash and half starving to death, don't you?"

"If it gets me stranded in a cozy cabin in front of a fire with someone like Jake, I'll take it." Shelly motioned up and down Jake's body.

He heard Rafe guffaw off stage.

Chloe saved him from the embarrassing comments by taking his hand. "Jake's amazing. I'm so blessed he wants to keep me around with how much trouble I've been so far."

He lifted her hand and kissed it. "Most exciting

assignment I've ever had. She had my heart racing long before the plane crashed."

The crowd ahhed. Jake clung to Chloe's fingers as Shelly and Brian asked a few more questions. She rubbed slow circles on his skin with her thumb. Her hand trembled slightly, so he wasn't sure if the motion was to calm herself or him.

The interview ended, and Chloe took the stage with her band. He blew out a quick huff of relief and went back to stand next to Rafe. Jake couldn't even bring himself to scowl. As Chloe sang a song about a romance that flew to the skies, he knew he'd crashed hard into love. A smile spread across his face, filled with a fullness he never thought he'd feel again.

EPILOGUE

Rafe's gut twisted as Jake sat next to Chloe and endured the interview. He never thought he'd see his friend emerge from the dark place he'd camped in since the mission. He hated when thoughts of that mission sprang up on him.

His hands trembled with the memory of taking a life much too young to be holding a rifle in battle. He shoved them into his pockets and rocked back on his heels. No use thinking about that right now.

He laughed as the spunky host hit on Jake. If Jake could put his beasts to rest and grab hold of life, could Rafe?

He peeked at Piper. She had her fingers over her cheeks, a beautiful smile stretched across her face. Her very being encompassed joy and innocence. He tore his gaze away.

Davis would kill Rafe if he knew the thoughts threading through his brain. Friends didn't cross that dating-sisters line. Rafe shook his head. What was he thinking?

He gazed back over at the interview, his stomach knotting. He wasn't like Jake.

Jake was a hero, taking a bullet for his friend and almost losing his life.

Rafe was nothing more than a child killer.

He closed his eyes, springing them open when all he saw was that adolescent boy he'd had to kill in the rescue mission that had gone wrong. No. Rafe deserved nothing but the false facade he put on to stop others from asking.

He chanced another glance at Piper. He definitely didn't deserve someone as pure and unsullied as Piper.

Rafe swallowed. He'd keep her safe until they could figure out who stalked her. Then he'd go back to his life at the ranch where he could bury himself in work and keep the jokester mask firmly in place.

Will Rafe be able to push aside his regrets and accept Piper's love, or will the hauntings of his past leave her brokenhearted again? Find out in Discovering Rafe, the fifth book in the Stryker Security Force series.

ALSO BY SARA BLACKARD

Vestige in Time Series

Vestige of Power

Vestige of Hope

Vestige of Legacy

Vestige of Courage

Stryker Security Force Series

Mission Out of Control

Falling For Zeke

Capturing Sosimo

Celebrating Tina

Crashing Into Jake

Discovering Rafe

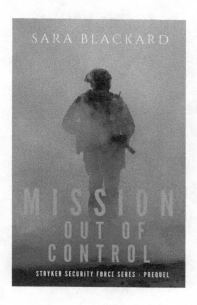

It was a mission like any other ... until it blew apart around them.

When the Army's Special Ops team is tasked with infiltrating the Columbian jungle and rescuing a kidnapped State Department family, the mission seems like every other one they've executed. But as the assignment unravels, not only is the mission's success at stake, but all the brothers-in-arms leaving the jungle alive hangs in the balance.

Mission Out of Control is the prequel short story for both Vestige in Hope and the Stryker Security Force Series.

www.sarablackard.com

ABOUT THE AUTHOR

Sara Blackard has been a writer since she was able to hold a pencil. When she's not crafting wild adventures and sweet romances, she's homeschooling her five children, keeping their off-grid house running, or enjoying the Alaskan lifestyle she and her husband love.

CPSIA information can be obtained
at www.ICGtesting.com
Printed in the USA
BVHW082041060122
625603BV00005B/93